CH00739388

KILLERPEDE

MAREK Z. TURNER

SEVERED PRESS
HOBART TASMANIA

KILLERPEDE

Copyright © 2022 Marek Z. Turner
Copyright © 2022 by Severed Press

WWW.SEVEREDPRESS.COM

All rights reserved. No part of this book may be reproduced or transmitted in any form or by any electronic or mechanical means, including photocopying, recording or by any information and retrieval system, without the written permission of the publisher and author, except where permitted by law.
This novel is a work of fiction. Names, characters, places and incidents are the product of the author's imagination, or are used fictitiously. Any resemblance to actual events, locales or persons, living or dead, is purely coincidental.

ISBN: 978-1-922861-09-2

All rights reserved.

PROLOGUE

"The stars are so romantic, don't you think?" said Mercedes. She smiled as she laid on the grass hill overlooking the recently opened quarry.

"Yeah, yeah, I agree babe," said Scott next to her, as he moved a hand to the zip of his tatty jeans.

Mercedes moved onto her side and stared at him. "Why did we come here, instead of going to the beach?"

Under her gaze, Scott readjusted himself and continued to look up. Right now, eye contact wasn't his friend. Should he tell her the truth? What would that achieve? "I thought it would be more romantic. Just the two of us here. Together in the universe."

Mercedes looked at the sky again. "I knew a real man like you would know how to treat a woman like me. I can't tell you how pleased I am to not be taken out to another fast food place. Are we going for a nice meal after this?"

"Yeah, of course we are," said Scott with a smile, knowing full well his mate was going to call with a fake emergency and require his help. He couldn't believe that she swallowed that answer, and with last week's storm turning the entire area into a mobile phone dead spot, he knew there was nothing to stop him getting what he came for. His right hand returned to his jeans, while his eyes watched Mercedes' pert breasts move up and down with her breath.

It was time to make his move. He rolled on top of her and lifted her short pleather skirt. "Come on, there's no one here. Only you, me, and the stars baby girl."

From their text conversations, he knew she loved it when he called her that, but truth be told, with her being seventeen years his junior, it made him feel creepy. Still, if it meant he got off, it had to be done.

"Wait, one second," said Mercedes as she placed a palm on Scott's chest. "When did you realise you loved me?"

A huge lump formed in Scott's throat, and he had to be careful what he said. "Baby, the first time I saw you walk out on that pitch in those little shorts, I felt it. You were magnificent that day. The way you handled those balls. I was proud to be your coach, and now I'm proud to be your lover."

Mercedes looked at him and smiled. Scott took that as consent and fumbled with her black underwear. He couldn't believe his luck and certainly would not let this opportunity get away. Within just two weeks, he had gone from being the lowly assistant manager of the local convenience store to being a respected member of the community who helps coach the local school girls football team. If anyone found out about this, like his wife and daughter, then all that would go and he would be left with nothing. So, he best get on with it.

Within moments, he was inside her and thrusting, gyrating, and groaning.

Mercedes remained there, impassive. She tilted her head and noticed a slight movement in the nearby bushes.

Scott thrusted harder and faster, oblivious to his partner's lack of involvement, as Mercedes kept her focus on a single shrub that shook in the night's stillness.

"You nearly there, baby? I'm nearly there," grunted Scott. It was like he was in a porno and he was the star.

Mercedes closed her eyes.

"Oh, what's that? Kinky stuff, eh," said Scott, as a light tickling sensation made its way up the back of his thighs. The unusual, almost massaging sensation of what he thought must have been fingers made its way up to his butt and slightly parted his cheeks.

"That's it. Shove a finger in there."

"What are you talking about? Just finish," said Mercedes.

Scott opened his eyes and saw Mercedes had her hands out to her side. The light touching of his ass continued, only now he realised that the gentle probing was all down his right hamstring as well. He froze as tens of tiny little things tapped at his skin and probed around his asshole.

Then it was as if his rectum was Mount Vesuvius and a searing hot pain roared up into his colon.

He howled into Mercedes' face, covering it in spittle as he ejaculated into her vagina. The semen dripped out of her and joined the fresh red blood that flowed from Scott's torn anus.

Mercedes pushed the gibbering and crying man off her. *What was his problem?* She watched as he thrashed around, and it was on the third roll that the cause of the horror became apparent. A giant creature was stuck up his ass. Its long body jerked about along with its host. Then Scott went still.

A foul stench pervaded the night as Scott's bowels evacuated and flushed the creature's head out in a tidal wave of rust-coloured excrement.

Mercedes got up and ran. Her legs wobbled on the impractical three-inch heels she had worn and within a matter of seconds, her right foot bounced back off the shell of a small creature hidden in the darkness.

The ground rushed up to her face, and her chin connected with the hard ground. The thud reverberated through her skull and her vision blurred. Then her senses returned.

Several carnivorous arthropods swarmed Mercedes, their venom bearing front limbs leaving small puncture holes behind them. The dirt encrusted shells traversed every part of her body, encasing her in a living coffin.

Despite the searing pain, she had remained conscious. Though she soon wished she hadn't. A fat, pungent creature clambered off her face and down her back, leaving a clear view of an enormous creature scuttling straight towards her.

She opened her mouth to scream.

CHAPTER 1

A fist slammed down on the small circular table and caused the top of Russ's pint of bitter to spill over. The old man looked up at the red face of Marlene Boggs and tutted as he shook his head. *When did society become so nasty? Back in his day, you showed respect to your elders, at least in public*, he thought.

"Wot' did yoo say?" spat Marlene Boggs, a Friday night regular in the Pulled Pork pub.

"Yeah, I dare you to say it again," said a man with a northern accent, London perhaps, and dressed in a suit. He stood behind Marlene and was no doubt only here for the weekend. Which was about as long as Marlene kept her men around. It's no wonder her daughter turned out the same way with that moral compass to guide her.

"I simply commented that it was likely that she had gone off with a man, and will turn up when they get bored with each other, as the youth of today are wont to do," said Russ.

"Wot' would yoo know? You lonely git. My Mercedes ain't like that. She's a good girl, salt of the earth. Besides, she would never miss pound-a-pint night with her maa. You're just jealous that no one would miss you. You ain't got nobody. Every time you're in here, I see you sat in this dark corner, with only your mangy mutt for company."

"The reason for that, madam, is that you are always in here." Russ felt a pang of sorrow at what Marlene had said, and he had to admit there was a hint of truth to it. However, he *had* been blessed with a good life and a wonderful family, and he hoped to see them again soon. The thoughts took his mind to a happier place, and so he did not notice that Marlene's face had turned almost a purple hue and the fat digits attached to her right hand had grabbed the drink off the table.

In a flash, its contents had cascaded down his thinning grey hair and soaked his clothing. The small Cavalier King Charles Spaniel, resting at his side, looked at its master and whimpered as the obnoxious man in the suit let out a guffaw.

Russ searched around the pub, pleading with his eyes for support, but he only saw blank faces. Despite being born in the village of Chumleigh and returning with his late wife fifteen years ago, it was a room full of strangers. Youngsters with nothing to do but drink away the hours, second home owners who use the area as a status symbol and the odd person hanging onto life such as himself. No one spoke up for him. Quite the opposite, as some youths hurled insults his way until the owner told everyone to go about their own business and ordered Marlene and her latest squeeze to the other side of the bar.

"Here, you look like you need it," said a young girl as she placed a fresh pint and some napkins on the table in front of Russ.

"Thank you," said Russ before lifting the drink and taking a calming sip. "Sorry, but do I know you?"

"My name's Nita, I'm a journalist for *The Devon Times* and I wondered if I could ask you a few questions about the new quarry that just opened up, and what it means for the area. Will that be OK?"

"*The Devon Times*? Bloody rubbish. I stopped reading that a long time ago. Your lot sensationalise anything you can. Once I even saw a double page spread on how many bins were knocked over during the last storm. Still, it's better than when you just take comments off that internet site. What's it called? Titter? Twatter? I prefer my news reports to be informative and factual. Thank you very much."

"Yes, well, the website you are referring to is Twitter, and that is not what I do. Like I said, I'm here to report on the local quarry-"

"-A puff piece on that jumped up idiot who calls himself a businessman, I bet. You ever wonder how a quarry got given a green light and here most of all?"

Nita smiled. "Exactly. It's interesting that the businessman in question is also the chairman of the parish council, and with political connections, who all seem to have bought new cars. But yes, you are right. My boss sent me here to write a puff piece, but there is something much bigger going on. I'm interested in the impact it has had on the nearby wildlife, for example. That's why I wanted to get the views of residents like yourself, and of the XR camp down the road."

"I'm sorry, my dear, XR?"

"You know, XR, Extinction Rebellion. They are a non-violent environmental activist group and their camp here is growing day-by-day."

"So that's who those nice people who knocked on the door of my cottage were."

Nita smiled again and withdrew a small digital recorder, but Russ raised a hand. "No, let me please stop you there. If you think you are going to get a rant from a long in the tooth curmudgeon, then you are very much mistaken. I came here just to have a nice ale in silence. I appreciate the drink, but as you bought it, hoping for something in return, I must decline and bid you goodnight," said Russ as he looked down at the half asleep dog.

"But, no wait, you have it all wrong," said Nita.

Russ struggled to his feet and at the almost painful click of his fingers, his faithful companion Toby did the same. He pulled open the large oak doors to a chorus of jeers. Community spirit is dead, he thought, and he stepped out into the frosty night.

CHAPTER 2

"Ignore him, my luvver. He's just funny like that," said a scruffily dressed man perched on the edge of a bar stool.

Nita felt her muscles tense as she glowered at the guy who remained staring at her. She would expect that sort of attitude down Wetherspoons, but not in a village pub.

"I am not your lover!"

The man put his hands up in mock surrender and gave a broad smile. "No offence meant, it's how we talk down here." He smiled and looked sincere.

"I'm sorry," said Nita. She didn't want to come across as naive or rude, especially before getting anything she could use in her story. At university, she learned that if you ever wanted to see the genuine picture, it was important to fit in and earn trust. That meant knowing the lingo and being seen as one of them. Although with her permanently tanned skin, it was a little hard to blend into these small, rural Devonshire communities.

"It's alright, so where are you from then? I can tell you aren't from here."

"Leicester, in the midlands. I came down here for university, and just fell in love with the county."

"Yeah, it is something special here. Now, hope you don't mind me asking, but where are you really from? Your family, I mean."

"India. Why?"

"Just curious. I love a good curry. Great food. Anyway, you wouldn't have gotten much out of old Russ there anyhow. That man has suffered and you can tell. Few years back, his wife headed out for a walk and when she never returned, poor Russ went out looking. He found her lying dead on the ground. Heart attack or stroke or something. Horrible. Come to think of it, it happened near to where the quarry is now. Anyway, if that wasn't bad enough, his only son died shortly after that. Ever since, he shut himself away and spends all day wallowing in pity at Moss Manor."

"Where?"

"That cottage of his. He calls it *Moss Manor*, but what good is a beautiful place if you spend your time there drowning in grief? The only break the poor grump gives himself is when he drags himself in here to do the same, but with different wallpaper." The man patted a dirty hand on the empty bar stool next to him. Nita took him up on the offer. "Now, did you say you were a journalist?"

"Yes, I'm here to write about the new quarry, and its impact on the community." Nita placed her recorder on the bar.

"Then you're speaking to the right man. Peter Pengelly's my name, and I've lived here for all of my seventy-odd years of my life. That godforsaken eyesore has brought nothing but misfortune to this village. It has upset the natural order. Now, a lot of you youngsters scoff, but there are things living under these here rocks - piskies, as old as time itself."

"I'm sorry, piskies?"

"Small, little creatures. You probably know them as pixies. Here, they live out on the wild land, and if you stood amongst the stones, you used to hear the song of the piskies, but not no more. Like in the nearby town of Ottery St. Mary, where the Church destroyed their dominion. They have put a curse on this place and we are all doomed!"

Nita moved a hand up to her mouth and did her best to stifle a laugh.

"You think it's rubbish, eh? Superstitious nonsense. Well, ever since that damned place opened last week, people's pets have been going missing. Hell, even the gulls have stopped coming around. Something's spooked 'em. It's the piskies looking for revenge."

"I'm sorry, no, but my focus was more on the environmental and economic impact of the quarry on the nearby residents."

"That's what I'm talking about. It has doomed us all. The only ones to get rich is that fat cat, Grant Hancock and his cronies. Meanwhile, we are all left to suffer. Mark my words!"

Nita returned her unused notepad and called the barman over. She ordered a pint for Peter Pengelly to thank him for his time and decided perhaps a pub in this strange village wasn't the best place to get a soundbite after all. Especially not when it appears that everyone has been on it for hours.

With an hour wasted, Nita hoped that her contact at the Extinction Rebellion camp would be a little more useful. They might exaggerate for their cause, but at least they won't be talking about bloody piskies.

CHAPTER 3

Grant Hancock eyed the thin man sitting in front of him. As the CEO of Chumleigh Quarry, he had a duty to make sure everything was working as it should be, and generating as much profit as he could squeeze out of the ground. So having this weasel stopping that was causing his blood pressure to rise. Apart from a stiff drink, the only thing that would help him now is if the little pillock replied positively.

"Not since Brexit. The rules have changed and these jobs just don't fit the new immigration criteria," said Bernard Williams, from across the lacquered meeting room table.

"Fuckin' hell, I've got lazy unproductive workers here and you're telling me I can't bring in some cheap eastern Europeans who would get the job done at half the price," said Hancock, as he slammed his cup of tea down.

"Even if we could bring them in, you would still need to pay the same wage, Sir, but it's not the pay that the employees are complaining about. It's something else, they say…"

"Humph. It's always about the bloody money, no matter what they say. Money makes this world go round and money, to the right people, will get me my workers. You will get me my workers."

Bernard stared at his boss.

"This wasn't what I voted for, Bernard," continued Hancock. "It was to keep our sovereignty and the right to keep the other lot out, not to restrict my bloody labour pool. Speaking of which, what am I paying you for, if not this?"

Hancock walked around the room and looked out of the large glass window that overlooked the quarry, his latest business venture. He glanced down at the empty pit but instead of seeing brown and grey colour slate, he saw his dwindling bank balance. He had bet big on the quarry's success and spent a significant amount in order to get the land and lobby the government for the relevant permits. That, he found out, was the simple part. However, he had underestimated the amount it would cost to get things operational. He needed to raise more cash. He had got a second mortgage on his house, but that was only enough to keep greasing the political cogs required to avoid any awkward or unnecessary questions. But in the current economic climate, the only backers he could find were not your traditional lenders who wanted him to jump through hoops to meet their standards of due diligence. Instead, he used the type of lender who would take a risk and, more importantly, ask no questions. As long as he made a success of the business, then it would be all good. And it would be successful, because thinking about the alternative would keep him up at night. If he failed to deliver, he faced more than just bankruptcy. His balls were on the line. Literally.

Now, in only five days he had suffered his first staff walkout, a bunch of crusty hippies had set up camp outside of the grounds and to top things off, this pillock, his so-called Chief Operating Officer, was giving only problems and not solutions.

He hired the mild-mannered Bernard Williams sight unseen because the man had come highly recommended. Had they met first, however, he never would have made the offer. Hell, even if he met Bernard one hour before the starting time, then he would have rescinded the contract. Such was the contempt Hancock held for the rule-abiding pencil pusher.

"OK, let's be sensible here then. If I can't get workers from Eastern Europe, I want you to look at India or Asia or wherever they earn pennies a day. I'll throw Tudor a few extra grand to grease the wheels of industry and see what he can swing with his contact down at the Home Office. In the meantime, we need to remove those soap dodgers outside and sort some positive spin about this place. When the bloody hell is this reporter meant to be coming? Invite him down to the pub tomorrow and we'll ply him with booze and force him to write about my generosity to the community."

"Well, she turned up earlier today, but you were in a meeting, so I dealt with it and told her to come back another time. It's only the regional press though, so I don't think it'll have much impact."

"Fucking hell, Bernard, must I do everything myself? Piss off home to your boyfriend and I'll give the paper a ring and get something pencilled in."

Hancock watched as his slightly built underling sighed and left the room. *Pillock*. Now, because of Bernard's incompetence, he had to spend his Friday night working. Perhaps he should get a secretary who could help him pass the time.

Standing alone in the silence, Hancock pulled out his mobile and dialled the number for Tudor, his local MP, and invited him to a meeting at the strip bar Temptations in Plymouth. It would be a bit of a drive and require him to spend on the company credit card, but this was how business was done. The quarry had to be re-opened soon, or he was fucked.

CHAPTER 4

Russ pulled back the net curtain and squinted out into the darkness of his long driveway. He really should install a security light, but why bother when he has his own form of protection? That and his eyesight was as clear as mud.

The first one-minute quick-fire round in *A Question of Sport* had just finished when he heard it. He thought nothing of it initially. Sure, it was strange for a seagull to be around at this time of night, but perhaps that is why it found itself in some distress. But when the squawking became louder, more desperate, he decided it was best to look. He hoped the badger problem that had blighted the area a couple of years ago had not returned.

It was this that ran through his mind as he stared into the blackness of the night. He was about to give up, but out of the corner of his eye, he sensed movement. He focused in on the spot and saw the white head of a gull rise from the gloom before crashing down to the ground. Enveloped by the darkness. The high-pitched cries remained, however.

Toby the Cavalier stirred from his comfortable bed, sniffed the air, and then waddled toward the front door of the cottage. He waited there and emitted a constant, low growl.

"What is it, boy? Badgers again?"

Russ joined his faithful companion at the door. He had no love for seagulls. The foul things were getting too cocky nowadays, but he couldn't let one get ripped apart.

He looked at his Wellington boots but went for comfort. After slipping his feet into his Harris Tweed slippers, he opened the door as far as the latch chain would allow him. Once again, he peered out into the nothingness.

The noises continued, and Russ felt the desperation in the gull's cries. He unhooked the chain from the latch and opened the door a little wider. With a movement that belied his age, Toby the spaniel rushed out of the doorway and down the gravel driveway. He disappeared into the night with only his barking to follow.

Russ put on his padded Barbour jacket and followed the noise.

He stopped suddenly as the night went still and he could hear only his own laboured breathing.

His body stiffened as a high-pitched yelp tore through the silence and threatened to pierce his eardrums.

The old man called out to his lifelong friend. Nothing. He returned to the house and made for the storage cupboard in the entrance hallway and withdrew a 20 gauge shotgun. Then his liver-spotted hands tipped over a box of three-inch shells and dropped three into the weapon. Ready to face the bloody badgers and get Toby back, Russ stepped out into the abyss. His ears noted no seagull and no Toby, although with his hearing, it didn't mean anything. As he made his way down the driveway, his ears picked up a strange noise that he couldn't quite work out. He paused and listened.

Slurp. Sluuuurp. Slurp.

"Is anyone there? Toby?"

Russ chuckled to himself. Did he really expect Toby to say something back? No, but he could have barked at least.

The clouds parted, allowing the moonlight to shine down and illuminate part of the driveway. It was then he saw it. It laid there on the boundary between the light and the dark, but it was unmistakable. A gull ripped in half. Its crimson blood contrasted the grey gravel.

"Toby? Toby!"

Russ raised his shotgun and waited. His mind could not make sense of what he saw. Badgers were vicious bastards, but he had never seen that before. An icy breeze carried with it the faint sound of barking and gave him the chills. He swept the gun around in a semi-circular motion as he shuffled backwards into the cottage.

The silence was absolute.

CHAPTER 5

Music blared out from the speakers of the old Fiesta as it rattled along the dark, narrow country lane, hemmed in by large imposing hedges. Nita strained forward so the top part of her body was practically over the steering wheel, as she navigated the road and tried to spot the turns before the vehicle's headlights brought them into immediate view. The countryside system of beeping your horn on every corner seemed a little silly to her, especially at this time of night. She was best off just being vigilant.

Nita grimaced as she took another sharp bend, and then she breathed a sigh of relief as a road sign for the quarry appeared. She smiled at making it without incident. Being a city girl, one thing she would never get used to were the perilous country roads. Her thoughts turned to having a cigarette when she reached her destination. *No, no more.*

The suspension on the car compressed, and the vehicle groaned as Nita lifted off her seat and her eyes widened. A deep thud reverberated throughout the vehicle and caused her to let out a small yelp. She slammed her right foot on the brake and jerked forward.

She sat there for a moment in silence. Her chest ached, and it took her three attempts to undo the constricting seatbelt. She rubbed the back of her neck. *What did I hit?*

Nita exhaled deeply and then looked into the rear-view mirror. She frowned. The distance covered by the lights was nonexistent, as a thick fog had shrouded the lane in a mysterious nothingness.

It would have been easier to just continue on to the Extinction Rebellion camp and the quarry. To forget about this. After all, it was likely to only be a stone or a branch or something. At worst, a rabbit or some other small animal. That thought made Nita think of her childhood pet, Mr. Flopsy. If he was outside and hit by a car, she would have wanted someone to at least check on him.

With a trembling finger, she flicked on the courtesy light and then rummaged around in the glove box, pulling out an LED torch and a packet of cigarettes. She needed both in this situation. It was only after killing the engine and the radio with it she heard the noise.

My god, she did hit something.

Her hands trembled as she opened the car door, the thought of a smoke evaporating in her mind. Her torch swayed from side to side, highlighting pockets of the road, until she saw a crumpled mound on the tarmac.

The beam and her body froze. She watched the mound lightly rise and fall until it emitted a low raspy groan and fell silent. Driven by some unknown compulsion, Nita stepped forward to see what it was.

Beneath the blood, the shape took a recognisable form. An old Cavalier King Charles Spaniel.

"I'm so sorry, boy. Don't be dead."

Nita crouched down beside the animal and noticed small wounds around its legs and chest. She stared at the strange cuts and tilted her head. If she had hit this poor dog, it would be an impact wound, maybe a broken leg or something. Not this. Nita placed a hand on the creature's side, its fur matted down with blood, and felt the weak beat of life.

"Yes, boy, come on,' she said before letting out an uncontrolled laugh and shedding a tear. 'Where do you live? Let's see if we can get you home and patched up."

Nita sensed movement in the surrounding bushes. It seemed to be all around her. Closing in. The feeling of being watched grew. She scooped the creature up and rushed to the car.

She knew that there was only one other place nearby, and that the dog must have come from there. Even if it didn't, these rural people would know what to do.

She placed the animal down in the car's boot and covered it with her coat. She reversed back to the last turn and headed down the gravel driveway to the cottage. Thank fuck, the lights were still on.

CHAPTER 6

The shotgun rested against the wall next to the front room window. Russ stood as still as a statue, staring out and waiting for Toby to return.

Dazzling lights split the darkness and caused the old man to blink. He glanced down at his watch and wondered who would visit him at this hour? It certainly wasn't someone coming for a friendly chat. His skin turned cold as he thought about the last time he received a visitor so late at night. It was never good news.

The car roared down the driveway, spraying gravel around its wheels, and came to an abrupt stop only metres from the cottage. Russ reached for the shotgun and went to meet the stranger.

He cracked the front door open, keeping the safety chain on, and waited for movement. The weapon hidden beside him.

The car horn blared and gave Russ a start. He had been daydreaming. It was happening more and more frequently. He blinked and stared at the vehicle. The glare of its headlights obscured his view of the slight person who practically jumped out of the driver's side and rushed behind the vehicle. Was he about to be robbed? Perhaps he should have installed that safety light after all.

"Hello? You've got to help me. I've got an injured animal here. Anyone?"

Russ waited. It was a female voice. A strange accent. Clearly not local. However, at his age, you had to be careful. The criminals were getting cleverer, and he was unfortunately getting weaker.

The woman burst forward, carrying a dog. Toby. Russ's knees wobbled, and he placed a hand on the wall. No matter what this was, he had to get a grip and take the chance. He had the gun for protection, after all.

Russ fumbled with the lock. The damn cold must have seized up his joints. He got the door open and stepped out into the night, leaving the shotgun behind.

The woman moved toward him at speed, the limp dog in her arms.

"Toby! Toby! What have you done to my poor boy?"

"I didn't… I don't know," said the woman as sheglanced frantically around..

Russ could see the panic in her wide eyes. He recognised it. It was the look of someone not used to the eerie sounds that reverberated through the rural silence. Although, he had to admit that something seemed off about this.

"Bring him inside where it is warm, quick," said Russ, suppressing his desire to take Toby in his arms. He turned and shuffled back to the cottage.

In the front room, Russ looked into the glazed eyes of his trusted companion one last time before the old dog gave up the fight. He was now truly alone in this world. He clenched his jaw, took his friend and placed him down in the small bed that was by the fireplace. Then he cleared his throat.

"What happened?"

The woman didn't respond. She just stood there, motionless, looking out of the front window.

"I remember you. From the pub. What did you do to my Toby?"

There was no reaction.

Russ stamped a foot on the hardwood floor. The aftershock made his body tremble. His heart pounded, and he had a good mind to let her have it. Woman or not.

"They're outside. Whatever they are, they're here," said Nita, as she continued to stare out of the window.

Russ shuffled over and looked out onto the driveway. All he could make out was the compact car and some of the driveway that was caught in its headlights. He was about to speak, to tell her what he thought of her, but then he saw it.

A strange creature scuttled across the beam of the left headlight. It must have been about two feet long. Badgers can be that size, Russ told himself, but he knew what was outside wasn't a badger. Then another beast appeared, and another.

"What are they?"

"They killed your dog. I'm certain," said Nita. Her eyes tracked the movement of the closest creature.

"Then I'll kill them!"

Russ hobbled back into the hallway and picked up his shotgun. He shook his legs, one at a time to get the circulation going, and checked his weapon.

"Wait, you can't go out there. We don't know what they are."

Russ grabbed the latch chain and steeled himself. He was ready to face whatever it was and whatever would happen to him.

CHAPTER 7

"We've got to call the police," said Nita.

Russ glanced back and saw her standing in the doorway between the front room and the hallway. She looked pale. Well, as pale as she could.

"There aren't any police out here. Quickest they can send someone will be at least an hour. If they turn up at all. Welcome to the countryside. We deal with our own problems," said Russ as he moved a hand over the doorknob.

"There's more of them out there. You can't go out, you're too old."

And I've got nothing else to live for, thought Russ. He sighed.

"The least I can do is get the buggers back for what they did to poor Toby."

Nita smiled at him. Russ did not know if it was sympathy or pity. It didn't matter, he supposed.

The abrasive sound of shattered glass brought them back to reality as fragments from the main window crashed down and covered the carpet with their sharp barbs. Nita turned toward the noise and her face contorted as her mouth opened and skin wrinkled.

Russ slammed the front door shut and shuffled towards his guest, who stood there frozen. He pushed past her to see what had happened and paused. Before them, wriggling on shards of glass, was a giant centipede. Its rounded head was smeared red and its elongated mandibles swung through the air, looking for prey to ensnare. It rolled over onto its back, exposing two pairs of maxillae bearing stubby sharp feelers.

It was as if Russ was watching all this happen to someone else. Without conscious thought, he stepped to the side to shield the young journalist and levelled his shotgun. He fired. The shot pierced the orange belly of the hideous overturned creature and chunks of flesh and goo exploded onto the surrounding furniture and walls. A small piece of matter landed on Russ' patterned slippers.

Nita screamed as two more of the creatures crawled in through the open gap of the window. Russ ejected the spent shell and took aim. The shotgun felt heavy and his arms ached. He fired again, hitting the rear of the closest creature. It was as if fire seared through his shoulder, but the pain was short-lived as adrenaline coursed through his blood, replacing the sensation.

He noticed Nita move into position behind him, facing the fireplace. Russ raised his weapon once more and blew out three pairs of legs from under another monster. The rest of the body flew backward and landed in a pile by the skirting board under the smashed window.

Russ readied the shotgun again and stepped forward. His head pounded and all he could hear was a loud buzzing in his ears. He pointed the barrel at the third creature, which had raised up onto its hind legs in defiance.

"Go back to hell," said Russ under his breath. He could feel his heart pounding like a jackhammer. His mouth was dry. Had his blood sugar levels dropped? His muscles were tight and yet weak. His finger trembled over the trigger. What was going on?

A cacophony of noises swirled around him. Screaming and screeching gave way to the loud deafening roar of the gun and once again blood, guts and grime redecorated the room.

Russ exhaled. The weapon fell from his hands and his legs buckled. It was over. He needed a rest. Some tea and maybe a biscuit for his diabetes. His mind momentarily fell blank. *It was nice to have company.* On his knees, Russ looked up to Nita for some form of encouragement, but there was only horror.

The woman stood in front of him, a fire poker raised and a distorted expression on her face. He knew never to trust people that turn up late at night. He closed his eyes and hoped that this would all blow over.

CHAPTER 8

It was like a tornado had spun Russ around as the young woman pushed past him and thrust the poker down to the ground. A raspy gurgle sounded behind him as she skewered the creature through one of its spiracles. As Nita pulled up the wrought iron object, it lifted the animal a few inches before the creature slid back down and hit the floor with a squelch.

But still it moved. It raised its upper body and emitted a death rattle akin to a grotesque wheeze, but as it did Nita rammed the poker straight down its pus filled maw. She screamed as she rammed it up and down, and with each strike, a few more chunks of viscera erupted out until only torn sinewy muscle remained.

Russ turned around and saw the parts of the creature's bloody head resting on his beige carpet. His eyes widened, and the last thing he remembered was the sound of heavy rain.

For a moment, Russ enjoyed the serenity of his unconscious state, where he was together with his family once more. His paradise was soon broken, and he hurtled back to earth.

"Hey, hey, are you still with me?" said a distant voice. "Shit, shit, shit. I don't need you to die on me, too. Why isn't there a bloody signal in this place?" continued the strange voice.

Russ woke with a start. His heart pounded, and his chest constricted, forcing him to take quick, shallow breaths. He stared at the room and the person in front of him but could not recognise either.

He wiped away what little sleep had congregated around his eyes and took in his surroundings. A cup of tea with a biscuit on the saucer rested on a small table beside him. His wedding day photograph was on the wall and above the fireplace was Paul's graduation photograph. The day *his* son became a doctor. Everything seemed normal. Perhaps he had left the radio on, passed out and had a nightmare. He sunk back into the comforting embrace of the armchair.

He was relaxing when he heard the creak of the door opening. He sat up as fast as his back would allow him to. The sudden movement kick-started a wave of fear and pain and his body suddenly felt heavy. His arms and shoulders ached all over.

"Who are you? I don't have much money," said Russ.

The woman looked at him and he saw concern on her face, which then turned into a welcoming smile.

"I'm Nita, the journalist. Do you remember me? Hmm, I should take you to a hospital."

"Why are you in my house? Toby!"

"Have some tea, and I'll tell you what happened. Are you sure you are OK? You look a little white…" said Nita as she picked up the nearby porcelain cup and saucer.

"I'm fine, my dear, just some bad dreams. Toby is gone, isn't he?" Russ looked at his sleeping companion, whose position had been undisturbed by all the ruckus. Russ' eyes then swept around what at first appeared to be his home but as his gaze moved past the fireplace and to the smashed window, the three dead creatures and a plethora of animal blood and gore, the full horror of the events of the evening returned to him. He waved away the drink.

"Where do you think they came from?" said Nita, following his gaze.

"I have no idea. Paignton Zoo, or perhaps someone imported them. I'll phone the police after all."

"There's no signal here."

Russ sighed. This was too much for him to take. Still, like in the past, he had to endure. For what else could he do? He struggled to his feet and headed toward the hallway telephone, which was hidden in a small side cupboard.

It took a couple of minutes of trying to explain the situation to the switchboard operator. They put him through to a call taker who noted the information, issued him an incident number and assigned an appointment for the following afternoon.

"No, you don't understand. I need someone now."

"I'm sorry, Sir, but unfortunately we cannot send an officer out to your location at present. If you are worried, I recommend you spend the night with a friend or relative. In the meantime, I'll also inform animal control and they will get in touch with you."

Russ slammed the phone down and shuffled back into the front room. Nita stood there expectantly.

"Not interested," said Russ as he shook his head. "No matter, I know who to phone. Do you mind getting my address book? It's over there by the overturned table."

Nita stepped over the detritus and located the small black notepad on the floor. A sticky, stringy pink goo dripped off it as she lifted it between her thumb and forefinger. She passed it to Russ, who had now regained his composure, and he took the book without a second glance. He paused and looked around the room before mumbling something.

"Oh no, this won't do. I've misplaced my glasses. I have another favour to ask. Could you come and read the names to me?"

"Crowson, P"

"Old-folks home."

"Carter, R"

"The wide one or the tall one?"

Nita looked at Russ and shrugged.

"Either way, both lost their marbles."

"Johnson, R."

"Ran off to Spain."

"Nelson. K."

"That's him. One of the few to make it. He lives nearby. I've not spoken to him for years, but I hear he's still raging against the light. Typical egghead. All the brains and none of the social skills to use it with."

"How can he help us?"

"He was some sort of bug expert. He'll tell us what to do. What's his number?"

Russ dialled and waited. He had just about had enough, when a cantankerous old voice answered and demanded if Russ knew what time it was.

CHAPTER 9

Russ and Nita shoved one creature into a duffle bag, the only thing they found that would fit it, and put it into the boot of his Land Rover. He was proud to still have his licence, but wondered if it was time to let the DVLA know about his cataracts and joint problems. Things had changed in the fifty-odd years since he last took the test, but he felt safe to drive on these roads and that was all that mattered.

They drove slowly through the narrow lanes, and Russ made a point that this was because he had drunk a couple of pints earlier rather than admit it was because he couldn't see very far. At this time of night, even a person with terrific eyesight would struggle, but the rain was easing and within fifteen minutes they pulled up outside a large barn. Russ beeped the horn and a rotund man came out to meet them.

The man introduced himself as Doctor Nelson, and ushered them into his private laboratory, a converted space that shone like only polished stainless steel could.

Russ imagined this must all be very impressive to a young journalist. Perhaps it would have been more so had Nelson not been dressed in pyjamas and a dressing gown.

"We didn't wake you, I hope, Doc?"

"Well yes, you did, but I'm intrigued by what was so important. It better not just be a rabid badger."

"It's definitely not that," said Nita, before introducing herself and hauling the bag up onto the steel plate that rested on top of a table. The journalist puffed out her cheeks because of the exertion and then unzipped the bag.

Doc pulled on a pair of surgical gloves and pulled back the zip. He gasped and then looked at the two guests.

The three of them sat next to the investigation table and sipped on instant coffee. Russ thought the taste was horrible, but didn't want to say anything, not after the last time. Now it was just nice to have company.

"So, what's your opinion?" Russ nodded toward the lifeless creature that was on the table beside them.

"It's fascinating. A real gem. And you are saying there are two more of these back at your cottage? I… don't believe it. No one has ever found something this size. Not even in the depths of the jungle. I would like to do some tests in the morning if I may, then I'll phone some old colleagues of mine. This is all rather marvellous," said Doc.

"So, you've seen these creatures before?" Nita asked.

"Yes, Miss Mistry, but not quite like this. The *Scolopendra gigantea*, more commonly known as the Amazonian giant centipede, was my speciality. A fearsome creature. Fast and cunning. They look very similar to these, and were thought to be the biggest centipedes in the world, growing up to a foot. The Amazon provided ample prey, and that explained their length, but this magnificent specimen, well. Over twice the size and here in Devon!"

"Do you think someone brought it here? I don't see how anyone could get it through customs," said Nita.

She turned and saw Russ had fallen asleep in the chair and was snoring.

"Let him be. At our age, this is a lot to deal with. Well, my dear, the importation of exotic and in particular dangerous animals is big business so don't be surprised what can make it into this country. However, upon initial visual inspection, this does not appear to be the giant centipede we know and love. Perhaps this animal has always been here. They inhabit areas that are moist, warm, and have dark cavities in which these types of phobia-inspiring organisms often lurk. Devon is filled with these underground caves and crevices but how they would have stayed hidden for so many years makes that a fanciful possibility. Leave this creature with me, and I'll give you a report tomorrow afternoon. First things first, we could all do with some sleep."

Nita went over and placed a hand on Russ's shoulder and shook him awake.

"Thanks Doc, do I need to worry about more of them in the house?" said Russ.

"Well, I'm afraid to tell you that centipedes don't normally leave any evidence of being in your home. In fact, they often change their hiding place each day so I would say tonight you got lucky. I am, of course, talking about normal centipedes and their behaviour, but these are not your garden variety, so to speak, however looking at it, something tells me if one of these were still on your property, you would know about it."

Russ looked over at his passenger and saw her stifle a yawn. He glanced at the clock in the car. 02:47. It had been a long night.

"If you can't get back to wherever you are staying tonight, you are welcome to stay in my cottage. I have a spare room which is already made up."

Nita smiled and said thank you, but Russ knew she was doing him the favour. *What if those things returned?*

CHAPTER 10

"Billy, Billy, wake up. Please," said Georgie.

"What? I'm trying to sleep here."

"There's something outside. I'm scared."

Billy huffed, unzipped his sleeping bag, and sat up. He yawned as he stretched his hands out and reached for his mobile. Dead battery. Perhaps it was his fault, but he had so few opportunities to watch videos online without his parents being just a room away. He threw the phone down, picked up a torch, and turned to face his younger brother. It was almost enjoyable to see the fear in his eyes.

"Maybe it's the Hell Hound. Come to take you back to the underworld," said Billy as he shone the light up from under his chin, casting a demonic image. He laughed, but as Georgie's lower lip wobbled, Billy felt the gnawing sensation of guilt in his head.

The brothers were four years apart, and with that, Billy believed he was too mature to be hanging out with his nine-year-old brother. However, after a recent fight, their parents insisted they go on a small camping trip together and rediscover being friends. And Billy had to admit that despite his sibling being too childish for him now, they had fun. Although, he would have preferred that they had it on a night when everyone else wasn't hanging out in the village square and watching the dressed-up older girls going to the pub.

"Look, it's probably nothing more scary than a curious rabbit checking out our cool tent."

Then Billy heard it. At first it was light scuttling from behind where Georgie sat, but soon the noise circled them. As it moved, the boys followed the noise with their eyes. After one lap, they noticed that the fabric of the tent was being pinched. Their fortress was being tested.

Billy and George huddled together in the centre of their polyester castle and prayed.

The movement outside grew louder, more frantic, as if more things were circling them.

Georgie let out a cry that turned into a full on blubber as he begged for his mummy.

Framed by the moonlight, a monstrous silhouette rose on its hind legs and sounded an unholy hiss. The outline towered over the tent and froze momentarily. The boys sucked in all the air around them. Then the creaturecrashed forward with ferocious speed, pushing down against the closed entrance flap.

Both boys screamed, and the creature flung its entire body against the thin fabric. The only thing between it and them. As the weight of the monster pushed against the plastic cover, the supporting plastic poles creaked and bent, forcing the tent to compress in on itself.

More of the things clambered onto the tent's surface, forcing its thin nylon sides to press down against the ground and trapping the boys in a small pocket of space.

Billy grabbed the torch and shone it straight at the entrance. The powerful light broke through the cheap plastic, and the enormous creature recoiled.

"You did it! Shine the light at them," screamed Georgie.

Billy swung the torch around and pointed it at each side. The creatures retreated.

Silence.

Inside, it stank of urine, but the boys did not move from their position. Better to stink than be dead, thought Billy. A nervous laughter erupted from them as they bathed the tent in a beam of light.

They sat there, illuminated by the maglite their father had bought them, and felt secure. Even if those things came back, they were ready.

Then the light flickered. Billy and Georgie looked at each other. Their faces pale.

"Are we able to go home now, you think?"

"Perhaps we should wait a little longer. It's safer," said Billy.

"I don't wanna. What if the torch stops? Let's go home. I want my bed, and my Mummy. Can we run home?"

"I know it's not far, but it's dark."

"If we go now, then we still have the magic torch," said Georgie. He smiled. "You are like a Jedi, and this is a real lightsaber defeating the baddies."

"OK, let's go for it. It'll probably last till we can get safe. Get your shoes on, leave everything else."

Billy took the batteries out of the light and put them back in the reverse order. That always buys a few more minutes of use. They unzipped the tent and looked around. No movement. They ran for it. The torch casting a new spotlight every couple of seconds.

They made it less than one hundred metres before a monster appeared before them.

CHAPTER 11

Doc Nelson flicked on the light to his laboratory, and whistled as he walked toward the work surface and the specimen that would do more than supplement his pension. His eyes, however, were fixed on the copious amount of Earl Grey tea that rode up the sides of the bone china cup with every step.

At the table he looked up and his mouth opened into the shape of an o. His bushy eyebrows raised, highlighting the deep creases of his forehead, and his hands trembled. A tsunami of tea covered his shoes and made its way out along the linoleum floor.

He didn't notice. All of his attention was on the empty work surface in front of him. After placing the cup and saucer down, he scanned the area. There was a light trail of slime that led down to the end of the table and around.

His heart beat like a jackhammer that was trying to break out of his chest, but the desire to know what had happened was too strong. After a deep breath, he followed the goo.

Bile rose in his throat and he had to use all of his control to keep it from going any further. He looked at the centipede. Disgorged, raw and torn into pieces.

Nelson cleared his throat and squeezed his legs together. He was worried that what little of his morning drink he had was about to make a reappearance. This was impossible. No creature could have gotten inside his laboratory. But something had done this. The creature was more or less in one piece on the slab last night. Wasn't it?

He placed both hands on a nearby stool to steady himself. His heartbeat drowned out all other noises. All except one. A disgusting high pitched slurping sound.

Nelson glanced around the immediate workspace and grabbed a portable bunsen burner. It was better to be safe than sorry, he reasoned. He switched the contraption on and approached the bloody pulp of the centipede.

"My God."

At the sight, his career flashed before his eyes. Only this time, he dared to dream of a future. He was once the pre-eminent arthropod specialist, sought throughout the world, but then newly qualified know-it-alls came in with their fancy other methods and technology, making his more practical skills and theoretical experience redundant. At his final meeting at the university, he was told that a machine could do most of what he did, and faster. With that one conversation, he had lost everything. His job and his self-worth.

These things, however, changed that. He not only had discovered a new species, but he had living specimens. This was his ticket back to the top. To become world famous again.

He put the bunsen burner onto the blue flame setting, placed it on the table, and then retreated towards some shelving that housed a series of beakers and other containers.

After selecting the right sized container for the job, he turned and faced his meal ticket. The creatures continued to feast on the flesh of their mother that they had dragged with them as they escaped from the decaying body, and Nelson was glad for their distraction. He knew centipedes could move fast and were agile. The element of surprise was his best bet.

After looking around the room, Nelson decided he stood the best chance with a frontal assault. There were three of the little buggers, but he only needed one. At least for now. After taking the lid off the container, he creeped forward.

He was within pouncing distance when the antennae of the closest creature swayed. The centipedes stopped feasting and lifted their heads. They moved into a triangle formation and then scattered. One climbed up the work table with such speed, Nelson struggled to track it. Another took to the wall and darted behind some shelving, but it was the one that didn't move that scared him the most.

It raised up onto its hind legs, showed its venom-bearing fangs and emitted a terrifying hiss.

Nelson dropped the container and reached for the bunsen burner. As his hand wrapped around the protective base, he felt a sharp stab of pain. He looked down to see the sharp claw of the second centipede attached. It was only a matter of seconds before the poison gland opened, if it hadn't already.

He gritted his teeth and prepared for his next move. Nelson had been in similar situations out in the field before. The trick was not to panic. With his free hand, he tried to pull the creature off, but it twisted its body and pressed its tiny legs into the soft, pudgy flesh of his arm.

His eyes shut before the first centipede reached his mouth and crawled inside.

CHAPTER 12

The dawn chorus woke Nita, and she stretched out her arms with a big smile. Sunshine had penetrated through the thin curtain and for a moment, she felt relaxed.

She sat up and looked around the strange room. Her gaze fell on her crumpled clothing and she realised she had gone to bed fully dressed. Although, that was also a bit of relief. She grabbed her phone off the floor and went to read her messages, but the only thing she could see was a tired face staring back at her.

After freshening up in the en-suite bathroom, she left the room and followed the happy-go-lucky humming that was coming from downstairs. She moved past the boarded up front room, with its stained carpet, and continued to follow the sound into the kitchen at the back of the cottage.

"Afternoon," said Russ with an enormous smile on his face.

"Afternoon? It's seven-fifteen.You don't have an iPhone charger, do you?" Nita sat down at the small, rounded table in the centre of the room.

"A what, love? I'm not sure what that is, but here is something better." Russ placed a large plate with a full English fry-up down in front of Nita. 'Would you also like some tea?'

Nita looked at the mound of food and wondered if it was just for her or if Russ had a whole family joining them?

Russ brought over two steaming cups and sat down. "Dig in."

"Are you not having any?"

"No, no, I ate my breakfast an hour and a half ago. I must say, after the initial horror of last night, I've been thinking about it and this is rather exciting. At my age, I get little to be excited about, but if I can stick it to those bastards who killed Toby, I will die happy."

Nita nearly choked on her tea at the language used by the old man.

"Well, I was planning to meet the XR activists, but my phone is dead and I can't check my messages. Although, considering what's happened, that's the least of my worries."

"The activists? Oh yes, lovely people. I hope they didn't get drenched a few nights ago."

"Could those creatures have come from there? I know you all believe in things living in the rocks."

"Ahh, I bet you've been speaking with Peter Pengelly. A nice enough man but a sandwich short of a picnic. While most people in these small communities grow up and spread their wings at some point in their lives, he never did and still harbours some superstitious belief in the myths of the area. If there were any rock creatures, piskies or ravenous centipedes, I think someone would have exploited them on TV by now. Don't you?"

Nita nodded. "I hope you don't mind me saying, but Peter mentioned something about the mysterious circumstances of your wife's death." Nita knew she had made an error of judgement as Russ's face turned vacant, if only for a moment.

"My wife died of a stroke while out walking. That's all there is to say about that!" Russ fired back, before standing up and moving toward the sink.

"I'm really sorry. I don't know why I brought that up," said Nita through a lump in her throat. She watched as Russ poured away his tea. "It's just the Doc was talking about how centipedes kill their prey and he also talked about the quarry. With what Peter said and that, I thought it a pretty big coincidence, that's all."

"Coincidence is just that, neither big nor small, but no, I can't see any link. I will admit that I found her on that heath, but you are forgetting one very important fact. The quarry wasn't even open back then. Now, how about you shower and get ready, then we'll drive over to Doc's. I'm sure he'll have something you can use to check your messages."

CHAPTER 13

Russ stood in disbelief as he watched Nita's trembling hands withdraw her mobile and photograph the scene. Doc was splayed out on the floor. His fingers gnarled and his mouth agape in a permanent grimace.

"What are you doing? Have some respect for the dead," said Russ, as the young girl moved around, capturing angle after angle of what had once been his friend.

"I'm sorry, but this is evidence, and if something is going on, then there is no way they can cover it up now."

"Cover what up? Why would anyone hide all this?"

"I don't know, but we can't be the only people alive who have seen them, can we? And what has anyone done to help? Nothing!"

Russ had to admit that she had a point, but there had to be a logical explanation for everything, including what had happened to Doc. The possibility that others knew about these creatures, people with the power to act but who did nothing, was almost as horrific as the monsters themselves.

Nita continued to press her point. "If I don't document this, then who will? Either we *are* the only ones who know about them, and then we have the responsibility to tell everyone… or this is some big sort of state secret and Doc died because we involved him. We owe it to him to expose the truth."

Russ shook his head. "No, you are just exploiting the situation and Doc's death for your own story. Cease at once."

Nita lowered her camera and looked at Russ.

There was nothing malicious about her intent, but what she was doing was inappropriate, and it was his duty to say so. There were right and wrong ways to bring about justice.

"Now, first things first,' said Russ. He took a second and tried to maintain a consistent level with his tone. 'We must call the police. They can't ignore this."

"No way, I'm not phoning them and getting caught up trying to explain all this. Besides, I need to submit some sort of story soon or I'll lose my job. You do it."

"I would, but I don't own a mobile."

"Use his landline," said Nita, as she pointed toward a phone that was in the corner. "Take my advice though, don't give them your name."

Russ dialled 999 and after explaining that he wasn't there when the death happened, and that it was likely caused by some kind of wild animal. Any more elaboration would have resulted in them labelling him as a crank. The person on the other end of the line agreed to dispatch a uniformed officer, and told Russ to stay there.

"I kept your name out of it, so you can go chase your story. I'll remain here," said Russ indignantly. "But before you go, could you help me look for some evidence which I could pass on to the Law?"

The two of them spent the next ten minutes in silence, looking around the laboratory for any clues about what happened, but they found little evidence other than trails of slime and small pieces of flesh.

Nita let out a loud sigh and moved back toward the bloated corpse. Her eyes narrowed as she stared down at the gaseous stomach. She inhaled sharply as a slight lump slowly appeared underneath Doc's lab coat.

The bump soon turned into an undulating wave that made its way up the rotund belly, past the chest and into the throat. She tried to scream, but she just stood there, her eyes transfixed and mouth open, as two antennae appeared from the gap between Doc's teeth.

CHAPTER 14

Police officer Callum Dick arrived at the cottage and pulled up next to the red Porsche Cayenne parked in the driveway. He exited the vehicle and surveyed the immediate area. The front door was wide open and, upon closer inspection, did not appear to have been forced. He lifted his hand to his radio and then lowered it.

In his four years on the force, he had seen very little action. Until now, his day-to-day consisted of dealing with angry farmers arguing over whose sheep were in whose field, helping lost and entitled tourists and the odd roughing up of a local kid for underage drinking. Hardly the thrills he had expected. No, this was his chance for some excitement. Some glory. But it would probably be a senile old man rambling on.

He tried to calm himself and repeated in his head that this was likely nothing more than a geriatric still living in the sixties and refusing to lock his door. Or worse, as the lads at the station told him, it was going to be a lonely fogey claiming to have spotted the Chumleigh equivalent of the beast of Bodmin moor or that cat on Exmoor. They had received a few hoax calls of that nature recently.

Despite trying to reassure himself, something about this situation didn't sit right with Dick.

"Hello? Mr Hamlyn, this is the police. Make yourself known please, Sir."

Dick stepped into the hallway, keeping one hand on his body cam, but his elbows remained tucked into his side in a defensive posture. Then a thought flashed through his mind. Perhaps it wasn't a hoax after all, but a setup. He had heard about criminal gangs luring lone officers into these types of situations where they would proceed to beat or kill them. In that moment, his stomach felt rock hard and he willed his bladder to remain tight.

The house was quiet, and the images of disgusting creepy crawlies that adorned the walls didn't help his anxiety. Nearby, glass shattered. He froze on the spot.

"Police. Come out with your hands up."

Silence.

Dick withdrew his collapsible baton and, with a flick of the wrist, armed himself with the weapon. Any assailant would have the element of surprise, but with his training and this piece of steel, he had confidence on his side. Or at least he hoped it looked that way.

The noises started again. It sounded like a burglary. But if it was still going on, where was Mr Hamlyn? *It's possible he was dead as well. That would be a shame, but a double murder could be a career defining case. A promotion too.* The Officer continued on until he found the source. *A laboratory. What the fuck, who has a laboratory?*

Pressed up against the wall, Dick glanced into the gap of the ajar door. There was no one. He peered in again, but for longer. Still nothing. Only the noise.

"Police, we have you surrounded."

No response. Only the crashing of containers and glass onto the floor.

The officer pulled open the door and entered the room.

CHAPTER 15

The laboratory was a mess. Scraps of paper, glass containers, and unspecified liquid covered the floor. Items had been knocked off the shelves and the work tops were covered in junk. A clear sign of a burglary.

Officer Dick's heart pounded. He paused as a near imperceptible breeze moved over him. Sensing the shift in the air, he tightened his grip on the collapsible baton and looked up.

There was barely time for him to comprehend the strange hissing sound as a giant centipede swung the upper half of its body down from above the door frame. Dick felt the thick, pungent shell crack into his nose.

As blood dripped out of his nostrils, he got a whiff of the putrid stench that emanated from the animal. It was like a decaying dog left out in the rain. The odour built until he could practically taste the thing on his tongue as it struggled for purchase over his head. His bladder loosened, and he became overcome with both warm relief and cold fear at the same time.

While his trousers flooded with urine, a wave of epinephrine swept through his body and the survival instinct kicked in. He swung both hands up to pull the monster off. The baton clattered against the floor. The creature squirmed, its endless legs poking and prying into his cheeks, but Dick got some purchase and pulled his face free, if only by a couple of inches. It was enough distance for his eyes to see the two claws in front of them. Then he saw nothing.

A searing pain ran through his nervous system. It was as if someone had electrocuted him. His nerves tingled, then burned, and his muscles stiffened. He dropped to his knees as the back portion of the centipede landed on the top of his cranium. Its legion of legs pinched into the sides of his fat head.

In his mind, he was begging for death, but the only thing that came for him were two more centipedes who caught him in a pincer movement and covered one thigh each.

Dick collapsed into a bloody heap, and the three creatures gorged on his paralysed body. His radio cackled, and a voice sounded out.

"PC 237, come in. Please state your location. Over."

CHAPTER 16

What was supposed to be a place of peace, tranquillity, and a chance for a brighter future had turned into the site of a massacre. Bodies lay scattered amongst the fallen branches and leaves, while those who thought they were safe in the tree houses fared little better.

It had all happened in a flash, and nothing could have prepared the members of the camp, which was populated with full-time activists, paid supporters, and weekend warriors, for what was about to come. Bulldozers, thugs and the obnoxious public had tried to stop *Extinction Rebellion* before, but never nature itself. It was ironic. A few days ago, they all rallied together and got through the downpour which practically flooded the area. That they could cope with. They even expected it in this country. But they could never have planned for a wave of ravenous giant centipedes.

Jude Briar was in the treehouse furthest away from the camp entrance, and by extension the quarry gates from where those creatures of hell spewed out. He was balls deep in a girl named Star, or Moonbeam, or some other crap when the screaming started. Briar, however, was no hardline activist, paid supporter or weekend warrior, but something altogether different. And Jude

Briar wasn't even his real name. It was a bloody awful name, he always thought, but he had been playing this game long enough to never miss a beat when someone called it.

Upon hearing the first scream, he continued his rhythmic thrusting, but as the noises outside overtook those from inside the cramped wooden space, he withdrew his penis and pulled on some jeans. His body slick with sweat, he moved to the window and brushed aside the net curtain with his calloused hands. There was carnage everywhere.

His muscles tensed. He took a deep breath and counted to two. Then a clarity returned to his thoughts.

"Get your clothes on, Star," said Briar, hoping he had guessed right.

"My name is Moonbeam. What's going on out there? Bulldozers already?"

"Do you want the good news or the bad news?' He smiled fleetingly. 'Just get fucking dressed, quick."

The last few chords of Wonderwall still hung in the air as the centipedes had swept through the unlucky activists who were sitting in a semi-circle in the campsite communal area. The clumsily played guitar and out of tune singing masked the rustling caused by the advancement of hundreds of tiny legs until the creatures crashed down on the eco-warriors in one gigantic wave. A tsunami of death.

They had crawled up the logs that substituted for benches and before the hippies knew what had happened, they had a giant centipede on their back. Meanwhile, those who were busy cooking a short distance away did not have time to react, as the speed of the coordinated attack took them by surprise. Pots and pans clattered onto the hard earth as hippies dropped paralysed to the floor, one after another.

However, the real horror was reserved for those unlucky few who were using the makeshift toilets. Constructed like an outhouse, but with a space for their feet to be visible, the centipedes scuttled under and caught their victims with their pants down. The smell drove them into a frenzy. Their antennas swung around, picking up the scent of shit, and they charged into the confined cubicles, scampered up the legs and poked, jabbed and stabbed the genitals of their prey.

Tobias Lennon was sitting in the third cubicle. He was suffering from a bout of indigestion after one too many halloumi skewers when the screams started. They grew in intensity and proximity until they reached a climax from the outhouse next door. He frantically glanced around the wooden box he was in. There was not even a plunger or cleaning brush. He settled his gaze on the only thing that he could use. Rolls of single-ply toilet roll. Then he had an idea.

He stood, pulled his pants and trousers up without wiping, and placed his bare feet on the damp toilet seat. His chances weren't great. After all, when did this ever work out for anyone in the movies but if there was a psycho, or worse yet a gang of psychos out there, it was worth a shot. Besides, he had to be back at Trinity College on Monday for lectures. If he missed any more, his father was going to reduce his monthly allowance.

With his pedicured feet resting on the seat, Tobias felt his stomach lurch. Not now, he thought. He needed to take his mind off it. And the screaming. He looked down at the pebble dashed bowl. His legs wobbled and the flimsy plastic creaked. In his head, all he could hear now was the grinding of his teeth. *Be quiet, they'll hear you. But they won't see your feet, you're safe.* He held his breath.

Then Tobias saw it. Or rather them. Tens of legs moving past the gap at the bottom of the door. Tiny, sharp limbs that pumped in perfect unison as whatever they belonged to moved about with ease.

Two of the things congregated outside the cubicle. *Please pass*, thought Tobias as he watched them turn, but he didn't know what way their strange ugly bodies were facing.

They struck with lightning speed.

Tobias swatted away the snapping mandible of the leading centipede, only for another one to climb onto him. His eyes bugged out at the sight of the hideous creature covering the whole of his arm. The creature wrapped its body around the thin flesh and sank its fangs into Tobias' soft, flabby bicep.

He felt the venom course through his veins and within moments, the heavy pressure that had weighed down on his body had disintegrated into a lightness that contrasted the darkness which clouded his vision. His feet slipped.

Briar headed across the rickety wooden bridge that connected two treehouses. He was certain that Moonbeam was close behind, but the force of his footsteps caused the walkway to swing violently from side to side.

Moonbeam grabbed one side of the rope railing with both hands and tried to steady herself. Nausea suffocated the back of her throat. She stood still and cried as a horde of centipedes swarmed up the two large black poplar trees that supported the walkway.

"C'mon, what the fucking hell are you doing? Man up," said Briar, as he turned back to the blubbering wreck that once infatuated him.

Through tear-stained eyes, Moonbeam looked at her former lover and then once again at the strange creatures that were making their way up the enormous trunks. Her crying turned into a wail and her knuckles turned white as she gripped the rope hard.

Briar glanced back at the approaching creatures and decided he had to act now. He darted into the wooden house and scanned the room for a weapon. Then a smile broke out over his face.

The joy was fleeting as a scream pierced his eardrums. He stepped outside just in time to see Moonbeam crash down into the dirt. Centipedes writhed atop her naked breasts.

CHAPTER 17

"I can't leave the situation as it is. Those demons killed my friend, and I am going to send them back to hell," said Russ. He picked up the car keys from his kitchen table and headed toward the front door. He stopped and disappeared for a couple of minutes into the cupboard space under the stairs. When he reemerged, he was carrying a large sports holdall.

"But you phoned the police. Let them handle it. If they don't, then I have evidence to take this to the top, and that will force them to act."

Russ did not look back, but continued towards his vehicle. He shoved the bag onto the backseat and then got in behind the wheel. Nita followed.

"That's if they even bothered to turn up. Besides, do you think a regular officer could deal with what we witnessed? No, what we need to do is for Doc, and for Toby," said Russ. He yanked the gear stick into first and pressed down on the accelerator. They moved through the lanes at twenty miles an hour.

"You just make sure you point that thing at them, and don't miss," said Russ as he released one hand from the wheel and pointed back toward the holdall. He had doubts that leaving the comfort of his home to return was the right decision, but when he returned to Moss Manor, and the mess caused by the centipedes, he knew there would be no safety until they dealt with the menace.

Nita looked at the old man and then stretched around to see what was inside. She unzipped it and stared at a couple of guns. As if sensing her confusion, Russ told her the one on top was a 686 Silver Pigeon shotgun. Nita said nothing in reply.

The Land Rover came to a stop next to the two other cars in the driveway, and Russ lowered himself down from the seat. He really needed a more practical car. That or to pick up yoga and gorge on cod liver tablets, but those things were foul, and his joints went stiff picking up the Sunday papers. How would he survive an exercise class? Still, none of that was necessary to fire a gun. He still had a good aim, and that was all that mattered.

"Nita, love, before you get out, can you get my spectacles from the glove box please?" he was glad he remembered.

"You need glasses for this?"

Russ noticed the doubt creeping into her face. Perhaps this was man's work and he should tell her to wait in the car. That would be the chivalrous thing to do, but who was he kidding? He's pushing on and could do with the help of a youngster.

After taking a couple of breaths, he took his 20 gauge from out of the bag and loaded it up. He then placed a few more shells in the pocket of his Barbour jacket and entered the building, hoping Nita would pick up her weapon and follow.

"Officer, it's Mr Hamlyn here, we're coming in."

"Shouldn't we be quiet in case those creatures are still somewhere in here? We don't want to alert them," said Nita, walking behind, her gun raised and swinging side to side as she moved.

Russ smiled. "True, but the last thing we want is for an officer of the law to surprise us and we pop off a shot by accident. I see it all the time with those dirtbag hunters. It's better if everything is out in the open. No messing about."

As the unlikely duo made their way through the hallway, Russ continued to call out. The loaded gun down by his side. Even in this position, though, the weight of the weapon sapped his strength, and he was desperate to put it down, but knew he had to endure.

They approached the door to the laboratory. Russ stopped short and Nita walked into his back, causing her right finger to tap against the cold metal of the trigger. She sucked in air and then coughed, releasing the pressure and loosening her grip.

Russ lifted a hand, but remained facing forwards. His eyes fixed on the two black boots that protruded from the door.

He raised his weapon and stepped forward. The gun trembled in his hands and he hoped his heart would take whatever he saw.

The inert body laid there. Its clothing was torn but bore the hallmarks of once being a police uniform. Russ breathed a sigh of relief and lowered the shotgun, which now felt more like a cannon.

Nita stepped past Russ, and after glancing at the horrified face of the body in front of them, moved around the room. The shotgun raised, and her finger poised over the trigger. She edged up toward Doc, whose lifeless and ravaged corpse remained in the corner. The body was thankfully devoid of creatures but the torn open mouth stared back at her.

"I think we're safe," mumbled Nita.

"What's that? I can't hear you."

"They're gone. And I'm no expert, but I'd say that they are bigger," said Nita. She crouched down below the level of the table top and when she re-emerged, Russ saw that between her thumb and her index finger, she held the shed skin of a centipede.

The two of them stared at the thin hollow scales and shuddered.

"Let's get to the village. We have to warn people," said Russ.

"Would anyone believe us?"

"It doesn't matter. Once the police or the army move in, they'll know it's true. Until then, we can only do what we can to tell everyone."

"Do you think the army will come?"

"It depends on what this poor soul told them. Either way, let's not waste time and get moving," said Russ, and he turned around without waiting for an answer.

CHAPTER 18

Nita stared out of the window as the large hedgerows turned into an equally bland, low, cobbled wall. Beyond that was just a blur. She was thankful that she had not had to use the gun, but also, she had to admit, a little disappointed to have not seen some action. What a story that would have been.

Her thoughts were interrupted as she realised Russ had been talking to her. 'What's that?'

"You think those things are intelligent?" said Russ.

"I don't know what to believe anymore," replied Nita, before sighing at the sight in front of them.

A flock of sheep blocked the narrow road and Russ bobbed his head from side-to-side, looking for their owner. After idling the Land Rover's engine for a couple of minutes, he turned the key, and the car fell silent.

Nita alighted from the vehicle and got some fresh air. The gentle bleating of the sheep, combined with the view afforded by the low wall, let her see all the way to the Plymouth Sound. She thought that in other circumstances, this would be idyllic. Far away from the traffic, pollution and greyness of the midlands.

It was then she spotted an old man walking in the field. He looked to have a stick and was poking the ground at random. "There's someone over there."

Nita pointed in the field's direction and watched as Russ leaned forward, as if advancing that minor distance would help his eyesight.

"Hmm, well, that should be Pengelly. I forgot he managed these fields. I bet he's to blame for these blasted sheep blocking the road, too. Look, there's an open gate," said Russ.

At that comment, Nita rushed off in the gate's direction. It was only fifty metres away, but it seemed to take her forever to reach it as the small cloud-like creatures jostled for space and in doing so knocked her one way, or forced her to turn another. The dream of a country life transformed into a nightmare of inconvenience and frustration. She made it to the field's entrance and called over to the man, who failed to respond to her shouts.

Her arms flailed as she ran across the uneven ground, and soon she found her hamstrings burning as she tried to manage her balance against the slight decline of the land. The blue expanse swallowed up the background as she approached the old man.

Pengelly walked with his head down, listening to Radio four on his portable player, while using his pointed stick to poke at the ground.

Nita called once more, but the man did not respond. Music blared from underneath his unkempt hair, so she placed a hand on the shoulder of the farmer.

Pengelly swung around with a speed and dexterity that defied his age and he raised the stick up, ready to pounce. Nita shrieked, and the noise caused the farmer to recoil.

"Oh it's you my dear. You must never sneak up on someone like that. Especially not if they are working a field," shouted Pengelly as he pulled off his headphones. "I'm sorry, you just startled me, that's all."

"No, it's my fault. I called out to you, but you didn't answer. So I came over."

"Now, what are you doing out in the middle of nowhere? It can't be for your story, can it? I've got nothing to do with the quarry."

"No, we were heading back to town, but the sheep are all over the road," said Nita as she pointed a finger toward the great white mass visible just outside of the field.

"Ah, yes, sorry, I was in such a state of worry I must have not shut the gate. There's something out here going round killing my livestock. The last few days I have lost seven of my flock. Stumped if I know what creature it could be."

"I think I might know what…."

Pengelly lifted a hand and waved a greeting. "So, you two made up, then?"

Nita raised an eyebrow at the man but ignored the question. He clearly wasn't all there. "We're heading to the village and you have to come with us."

"Russ," replied Pengelly.

"Peter."

Russ had joined Nita and taken a place to her left. The men nodded at each other and Nita, watching, had to do her best to stifle a laugh at the exchange.

"Listen, Russ, I'm sorry for not sticking up for you in the pub the other night. It's just… you understand."

"What's important now is that we warn as many people as possible," said Russ.

"About what? My animals? How did you know about that?"

Nita felt the conversation was going nowhere, and she didn't have the time to waste as the old men struggled to get to the real issue at hand..

"Listen, there are giant fucking bugs eating everyone they can, and by the sounds of it your sheep, too. We've got to warn the entire village before those things reach there," interrupted Nita.

Pengelly fell silent for a moment, then sprung into action. "Right, let's go to the pub then."

Nita and Russ stared at Pengelly as if he had just suggested a dereliction of duty.

"It's the town fayre today and there's a meat raffle tonight, sponsored by that nitwit from the quarry, a way to curry favour I suppose. No offence, my love. Everyone will be there already getting hammered, I bet," continued Pengelly.

That location keeps coming up, thought Nita.

A light breeze carried the scent of the creatures that hid in the surrounding green. The men, whose noses were attuned to the salt of the sea, the petrichor of the soil and the rather less alluring stench of the animals, sensed the shift in the natural order of things. Some smells, like petrol, don't belong in the idyllic countryside.

"Move, as fast as you can," said Russ, who, without waiting, had already turned to leave. Pengelly wasn't far behind him.

Nita tilted her head as she watched the two elderly men hobble with all their speed toward the car. She glanced back over the field, and then she understood. The unnatural movement of the grass and the high pitch of incessant hissing. She turned and ran.

Within seconds she had caught up with the men, and felt a pang of guilt as she heard their laboured breathing as she passed them with ease, but still she kept running. Someone had to get the car started. *Were the keys in the car?* The worry caused her to stop and turn.

She was about to ask about the keys when Russ disappeared. A grunt of pain made its way up to her ears, and she thought about her nan. How she fell and broke her hip. *Please God, don't let this be it for Russ. What about the keys?*

In that second, Nita had to choose. Russ grunted again. She burst back to help her new friend and, using all of her strength, hauled the old man up. She placed an arm around him and together they headed back to the car. Neither one dared look back.

As they slogged through the grass, the scarecrow-like figure of Pengelly got bigger as inch-by-inch they gained on him. Nita screamed for him to keep moving.

He didn't respond.

As they came level with him, Nita looked and saw that his right side had dropped, his mouth a half pout. It was then she noticed his entire body had slumped to one side.

A mumble fell from Pengelly's lips and, as Nita tried to decipher the words, Russ clarified it for her. Go! The two of them hobbled on, leaving Pengelly to stumble on a left turn and shake his walking stick at the oncoming horde.

The centipedes made light work of their meal; they covered the defenceless old man like white on rice. Their fangs cut through the old, weak flesh and the man succumbed to the poison almost immediately before becoming food for the swarm.

Nita and Russ heard no screams, only a low, wet slurping sound. The distraction granted by Pengelly had at least bought them the time to survive.

"You drive, my nerves are shot to hell. And my joints…" Through trembling hands, Russ offered the keys to Nita.

He didn't need to say any more. Nita grabbed them, hopped into the driver's seat and fired up the engine, which roared over the near deafening bleating. She looked out of the side window, to the once peaceful field, and tears clouded her vision.

With one hand, she smashed the central pad of the steering wheel and the horn blared out. A couple of sheep glanced in her direction, but the rest ignored the warning. She let out a slight growl and set the vehicle in motion.

The Land Rover ploughed into the fluffy flock, shattering jaws and breaking ribs as it forced its way through. Nita glanced in the rearview mirror and the image reminded her of bloody cotton wool. It didn't matter; they had to reach the village at any cost.

CHAPTER 19

Despite the cold weather, several patrons braved the outside seating area of the Pulled Pork public house. They each stood with a pint in one hand and a cigarette in the other. Their vices lit up in a kaleidoscopic haze caused by the excessive multi-coloured lights inside the venue as music from the seventies escaped through every crack in the walls and doors.

"Eer, Russ, you grumpy git. Good to see you socialising again," said local MP Tudor Spears, who owned the largest house in the village but was rarely seen within two-hundred and fifty miles of the place. Spears widened his arms in a welcoming gesture. The movement caused the cloudy amber alcohol to slosh from his glass and onto the pavement.

Russ just walked past the man, whose reign with the Conservatives oversaw local funding cuts for the library, public transport, support classes and anything that didn't allow for expenses to be claimed from it, and entered the pub. Nita followed behind and poked her tongue out at the lazy, pompous freeloader.

Inside the old building, the party was in full swing. A temporary up stage took over the left-hand side of the bar, while the revellers and binge drinkers packed the right.

Those over the age of fifty smiled, nodded, and greeted Russ as he made his way through to the bar. Everyone else did as he suspected they always did, and ignored the elderly. He noticed, however, that several of the younger men did not ignore Nita. The look on their faces as they muttered to each other told him everything he needed to know about their sordid little conversations. Sadly, now wasn't the time to address that lack of respect.

"Stevie, you need to stop the party. Something serious has happened," said Russ to the landlord.

"Oh give over, Russ, we're just getting started. Whatever it is, can it wait until tomorrow? To show there's no hard feelings, have a pint on the house. Your girlfriend too," replied Stevie Wotton, with a hearty chuckle.

"No, it can't. Doc and Pengelly are dead! Send everyone home now."

"Old age, it gets us all. I understand why you'd be upset. If it helps, think of this as a wake. C'mon, have that drink."

"It wasn't old age, it was giant killer centipedes," said Russ. His body trembled with rage, or perhaps it was his blood sugar levels, or the fact he might have forgotten to take his medicine today - he couldn't remember. In that moment of uncertainty, Nita spoke up and supported his wild statement.

Stevie looked down as if deciding on what to do, before walking to the edge of the counter and ringing the antique bell that was usually reserved for last orders and free rounds. The hubbub reduced until it was a faint murmur and everyone faced Stevie with all the expectations that come with a pub announcement.

"Listen up, old Russ here is telling me we are all in danger… from man-eating bugs. Now, as we can't rely on the piskies to save us and Batman is busy cleaning up the streets of Exeter from all them there reprobates, there is only one thing we can do to stay safe. Have a lock in here!"

A loud roar of agreement echoed round the pub as Russ noticed the happy smirks of those standing around him. His attention fell on a group of lads in the corner who chanted and danced, making the floor sticky with spilled lager and the air stink with sweat. Although it wasn't their actions that interested Russ, but what was located next to them.

Nita followed his gaze, then looked back at Russ and nodded.

CHAPTER 20

Over three years of hard work nearly ruined by those hellish creatures, thought Briar as he glanced out from his hiding space in the small wooden hut. The camp had been silent for around an hour. It was surely safe by now. This wasn't what he had signed up for, nor ever expected. It surprised him to find that out of everything, it was his wife that entered his mind. How long must it have been since they were last together? And what about little Janet? Had he missed her fifth or sixth birthday?

A lump had formed in his throat, and he swallowed hard as his fingers wrapped around the handle of a short axe with one hand and he pulled back the curtain that masqueraded as a door with the other. Beads of sweat dripped down his grimy face as he surveyed the surroundings.

The woodland was quiet, and Briar breathed a sigh of relief.

He crept across the rickety bridge, but by the time he had reached halfway, his self-control deserted him and he looked down. Disgorged bodies and torn flesh littered the muddy ground. He felt his stomach churning the tofu and beans he had earlier and a sickly taste forced its way up to the top of his esophagus. It rested there, waiting for its moment. Then he saw the semi-naked body of Moonbeam. Her once beautiful skin now resembled the remnants of Christmas wrapping paper as flaps of skin flayed out in all directions from her disgorged carcass. His dinner made a re-appearance.

He regained his composure and continued on to his treehouse. Certain that the monsters had moved on, he tossed the mattress onto its side and pulled out a small secured case from a gap in the floorboard. After fiddling with the combination padlock, he took out an old mobile phone and called the only saved number.

"You gotta get me out of here. They're all dead. What the fuck happened?"

He heard a slow exhale, but no response.

"Weren't you watching? Why didn't you step in?"

"You have your orders, and I have mine. Now tell me, why are you calling?"

"What? You are asking me why? I told you, everyone's dead. Giant fucking creatures came from the woods and killed them all!"

"Get a hold of yourself, officer. Killer creatures, for fuck's sake, you're losing it. We overlooked your little trysts and drug taking in the past, but now you've gone off the deep end and it's compromising the mission. If you can't handle this assignment, I'll pull you out and make sure you do fucking traffic patrol for the rest of your career."

"Sir, send in immediate support and investigate. For Christ's sake, those things could be anywhere and there's a village nearby."

"I don't have to do shit. No one knows about this post apart from the Ministers, so there will be no assistance. As for your story about carnivorous ghoulies. Grow a pair and get the job done!"

The line went dead.

Briar threw the phone down onto the uneven wooden floor. He would need to head to the village and take care of this himself. Or at least grab a vehicle and get the fuck away.

CHAPTER 21

Russ stumbled up the small steps leading to the stage and thanked Nita for helping him up. He stepped toward the microphone like a man with authority and cleared his throat. A few people at the front turned to face him, no doubt intrigued by the oldest compere in the village, but most of the audience continued with their alcohol fuelled revelry, or more accurately, their loutish behaviour.

This chaos was alien to Russ, who grew up in the time of organised dances, and quiet, respectful drinking. At least in public. He shook that thought from his mind. The only thing that mattered now was that they came together to get through this. That they stepped up and met the challenge.

He steadied himself and spoke. Nothing.

Nita rushed across to the soundboard, which was located to the side of the stage, and pushed up the faders for the microphone and muted the music. A high-pitched whine fed back and in doing so caught the attention of the crowd, although more out of annoyance than interest.

"My fellow citizens of Chumleigh, you are all in danger. People are already dead, and many more will be if we don't act now."

Jeers rang out.

"Please, please listen. Giant centipedes killed Doc Nelson and Pengelly and have been mutilating livestock. Those of you with animals must have noticed something strange." Russ could sense the mood was changing, and he felt emboldened to continue. "Mrs Boggs, just the other day you said Mercedes was missing. When did you last speak with her?"

"Don't you talk about my Mercedes. First you call her a slut, now she's been eaten by giant bugs? You need professional help."

"Hear him out. I've lost at least ten sheep and three cows over the past few days and I have no clue what bloody animal did it," said Tennison, a powerfully built farmer who stood at the bar.

"Here, my dog Cujo, has been missing for about a week, too. Where did these things come from?"

Nita stepped up and took a position next to Russ on the stage. "We aren't sure, but this all started happening when the quarry opened. That is our best bet."

Nervous chatter broke out in pockets around the crowd as isolated incidents were compared and compounded to make a horrifying pattern. Within minutes panic flared, tensions rose, and the mob turned to direct their anger towards one man.

Bernard Williams looked up from his gin and edged his way away from the stage, but he did not get far and he found himself hemmed in by a group of large farmhands who had met the rallying call of that large oaf, Tennison. The whole cramped situation reminded him of being back on the underground in London.

He pointed his elbows out and made a little space for himself, but when the woman mentioned this all began with the quarry, Bernard tucked his elbows in and shrunk into a small pocket of space. The workers had been complaining to him since the place had started, and he had taken no notice. Of course, there was going to be some strange noises down there, as the hidden caves collapsed and the rocks ground against each other under the stress of the dynamite and machinery.

Besides, there wasn't anything he could do. The preliminary geographic reports were all paid for in more ways than one, and he was getting a good salary to ensure things not only got up and running, but remained that way. Sure, after listening to the workers, he should have pretended to make some changes. That would have at least stopped them from walking out, and he would own that mistake, although not to that shit, Hancock. Bernard honestly thought it was just an ecological issue. Something he didn't need to deal with. After all, he had genuine problems at home to sort out. Like paying that leech of an ex-wife and his kids' private school fees.

No, no, it wasn't his fault. The environment, OK, but who could have ever predicted something horrible was living under the ground?

''My God, Billy and Georgie were out camping near the quarry last night. Has anyone seen them today? Gregory, get your phone, call them," wailed Susan Derry, before she buried her head into the chest of her husband.

When the middle-aged woman started wailing about her kids, Bernard compulsively rubbed the back of his neck, causing his pint to tilt and splash on the people standing closest.

He apologised profusely and pushed his way through an agitated crowd, saying sorry more times than he had in a long time.

Bloody hell, those poor boys.

Then an icy shiver made its way down his back as a hush descended on the pub. There was a palpable sense of fear. Bernard stopped. Now, it was no longer the sweaty bodies that surrounded him that refused to let him leave but his own legs. In that moment, when his heart pounded like a hummingbird, a familiar voice boomed out from near the bar.

And Bernard smiled.

CHAPTER 22

Grant Hancock for once in his life baulked at being the centre of attention. He shifted on his bar seat as sweat trickled down his rounded head. The people formed a semi-circle around him and he knew when that happened, you had to have a clear exit path, else you were fucked.

However, he didn't make it this far without having made it through these sorts of situations. After counting to three, he turned and took a sip of his pint of ridiculously named craft lager. Now he was ready to face his accusers. But not before looking for that weasel Bernard. It would be a lot easier to pin this on him.

Shit. Hancock saw the wispy-haired loser working his way toward an exit and realised it would be on him to front up. He turned to look at the old man and the foreign woman standing on the stage and felt a bit more confident about the situation. Perhaps this wouldn't be so difficult. The only time he'd ever really been under the cosh was when he was audited for tax fraud. He survived that and he'll bloody well survive whatever these prats had to say.

All he had to do was to discredit them. It never mattered what the truth was, just who people believed. As one of his pals once said, "the people of this country have had enough of experts", and he was right. Now it was time to test the water and gauge the crowd's initial mood.

"Has anyone here actually seen these killer creatures? No?" said Hancock as he plopped off his seat and walked towards the stage. He waved his hands as he continued to talk. "I have brought jobs to the village, money into the local businesses, and, of course, I paid for this whole celebration. Are you suggesting that I did all this to let loose a horde of ravenous creatures? Creatures to kill my staff, my customers and my friends?"

"It is a bit of a coincidence, isn't it?' said Nita. 'And isn't it also true that the environmental impact report was rushed through under suspicious circumstances?"

This girl had done her homework, thought Hancock. This could get messy if he didn't shut her up.

"You sound like one of those crusties up there disrupting my business and these fine peoples' livelihood. Let it be said that those hippies aren't here to help preserve our beautiful countryside, but they have come down here to disrupt our way of life and tell us we're all living wrong," Hancock pointed a finger at Russ. "And it looks like they have gotten to some of you. Older people, vulnerable people, those unable and those who are unwilling to embrace development and want to hold the rest of us and the village back."

The mutterings of agreement gave confidence to Hancock, who stepped up and now stood alongside Russ and Nita. Nita balled her fists and was about to speak, but Hancock would not give her the chance.

"Russ, here, is a member of our community, and I respect his age and experience, but it is time to move on. I bear him no ill will, just looking for company, I bet. He was likely manipulated by this, this visitor, who I don't know. Do you? Most likely she's here to cause trouble, to divide us. But we, ladies and gentlemen, cannot let her come here with her foreign ways and divide us. To upset our unity."

"I'm a journalist, and I know all about you, how you got the quarry green lit and the corners you cut…"

"Ahh, so you're the journalist, a most trustworthy profession," said Hancock with a sneer. "Now, let's return to the party. Landlord, drinks are on…"

"Billy! George! Quick, Susan, come 'ere, your kids are outside."

Susan Derry pushed her way through the packed revellers and shoved her face up against a grubby window. Her eyes widened as she saw her two beautiful children, caked in dirt, stumble down the narrow road and toward the pub. The smile that was etched on her face turned into a grimace.

"Just a few more steps, you can do it," said Billy as stumbled forward under the weight of his bloodstained and muddy clothing.

The second boy, Georgie, dropped to his knees. His descent only stopped when his jaw cracked the concrete. His horizontal body allowed the peering eyes to view the giant centipede that stood victorious over its prey.

Billy turned and looked at his little brother and then at the creature. His eyes rolled back.

Susan let out a piercing wail more grating than any feedback and collapsed into a pile on the floor. While those around her who still had their senses about them used their lucidity to engage in a quick-fire game of pass the message. The details, true and false, tore through the crowd as the witnesses garbled what they saw to the person behind them. Who, in turn, interpreted it and passed it back on. The news of a demonic child-eating monster reached Hancock and, with it, any chance of getting out of this unscathed evaporated. There are two things you should never mess with. Cats and children.

He sucked in the stale air and accepted, at least to himself, that perhaps there was a little truth to the story. They, the bloody experts, warned him about the cave system near the quarry, but the exploratory report said nothing about carnivorous creatures. There was the possibility of animals living there and that they would be displaced. It was par for the course. He obviously paid to get that section redacted, but this was something they should have told him about in private. He didn't like surprises.

It only took that moment of pondering for the devil to reach the door and for Hancock to realise that he was trapped inside with these morons. They would certainly blame him once they stopped their bleating. The only thing to do was to take matters into his own hands.

As the patrons shuffled around aimlessly, Hancock slipped off to the opposite side of the stage and through the doors to the toilets. Perhaps he could fit out the window. It would be tight, but he'd rather try than be killed by whatever was coming for them, or worse, the mob.

He opened the latch and, placing a foot on top of one urinal, pulled himself up to the rectangular window. Balanced precariously, he lifted his other foot up and made a mental note he would have to throw these shoes away once he was safe. He angled his body and pushed his head and shoulders through. It was then he felt it.

The tight frame squeezed his portly belly, its girth more than the space could accommodate. He tried to slide back, but found himself wedged in. Thoughts raced through his brain, the noise of them drowning everything else out. Everything except the hissing.

Below him waited three giant centipedes. They raised up onto their hind legs and continued to hiss. The sight and the sound combined made Hancock excrete his Michelin starred lunch from Lympstone Manor, and the brown sludge forced its way down his Ted Baker trousers and slopped into the urinal bowls.

Although wedged in, Hancock thought he was at least safe at this height. Then the first one started climbing the wall. It was soon joined by the second and the third.

CHAPTER 23

The main doors and windows creaked under the pressure of hundreds of probing legs. The continuous sound of scratching and tapping clawed its way under the skin of those trapped inside the pub.

Inside, the screams of the patrons grew in intensity and the high-pitched noise only seemed to whip the creatures outside further into a frenzy.

Everyone was so focused on the menace outside of the main entrance that no one realised a small train of critters had pushed through the bloated corpse of Hancock, who now lay slumped half in and out of the tight bathroom window. The putrid creatured made their way past the flimsy toilet swing doors, through the hallway and into the back of the main room.

It was Russ who noticed the movement of the door, as it first rattled, and then moved ajar despite no one being near it. His eyes remained fixed on the wobbling plastic door, but he could not focus on what he was seeing. Then the waving lines, the slight movements, and the antennae became clear.

"Nita, Nita, look," said Russ. He tried to hide the tremble in his voice, but knew the monsters had compromised their fortress. He raised a pale, liver-spotted finger and Nita followed its point. A scream broke free from her throat and she took a step back.

Her movement alerted the other patrons nearby, who turned in unison and saw the advancing arthropods. The group of people closest to the creatures bumped into each other in a desperate bid to escape, and in the melee, a middle-aged woman hit the dirty floor with a slap. Her head landed just thirty centimetres away from the leading centipede.

Russ grabbed Nita by the arm and pulled her back toward the sound desk. The centipedes swarmed the group at the other end of the stage and Russ knew their misfortune would buy them precious minutes to escape. If only he could think how?

In his younger days, he would have had the strength to force his way through the crowd and out of the doors. He might even have been able to bring some people with him and to send some of those crawling bastards back to hell. Not any more.

Despite his age, and failing physicality, his mind was still sharp, and he assessed the situation. People were packed against the exits, trying to keep those things out while silhouettes peppered the windows in temporary darkness.

"I can't take it anymore!" shouted Barry Johnson, and the young guy picked up a wooden stool and flung it at a large silhouette that covered almost half of the window nearest him. Russ screamed to stop, but it was too late.

The glass shattered, and the creature flew back into the street, only to be replaced by several more, which forced their way through the shards and clambered onto the vinyl seating under the window.

As more centipedes spewed through the broken front window, Russ noticed they had enacted a perfect pincer movement. They had to get out if they were to survive. There would be collateral damage, however. There always was. Russ glanced back at the innocent people that had already become bug food.

With their rears exposed, the front was the only way out. He told Nita in no uncertain terms what they had to do and the two of them shouted instructions as they moved forward toward the main entrance. They just had to hope that it would work.

As they got closer to the door, the space available reduced, and Russ found himself pushed aside and separated from Nita. His voice cracked and his throat became raw as he continued to shout. The crowd, however, cast him aside, and he fell back behind those younger or stronger who had latched onto his plan for themselves. He became an island in a sea of desperation. Perhaps this was how it ended. Discarded by those he had tried to help. He glanced up and looked for Nita.

The young woman had climbed onto a seat and stood above everyone. Her tone was strong and authoritative. "Our only way is to make a run for it. They're only bugs. Let's open the door and rush them. They won't expect it and we'll have the advantage. Kick them if you have to, but don't stop moving until you reach safety."

Shouts of support mingled with fear and uncertainty, but then hands gripped the handles and pulled the door wide open. The choice was made. The crowd surged and screamed as they burst out into the street. Nita jumped down, moved around the thinning crowd and took Russ by the elbow. He felt her lead him along with the current and he couldn't help but smile that she had come back for him.

The gloomy lighting of the pub gave way to an eerie, cloudless evening. Russ struggled to process the sensory overload. Screams and shouts swirled around him, incomprehensible. While his eyes took in horrific sights everywhere they looked. They widened as shaggy-haired Patrick Mulligan stumbled in front of him, writhing in terror as a giant centipede had wrapped its elongated body around his neck and its gaping maw prepared to chomp on its victim's bloated, red nose.

Mercifully, Russ failed to hear the screams as the bells from the local Trappist monastery tolled. A force dragged him out of his stupor and his legs moved almost automatically. He imagined he was back on Goose Green and took solace from the result of that day. The next thing he knew, he was sitting in the passenger seat of the Land Rover and heading south at speed.

CHAPTER 24

Father Keating stood at the bottom of the tower and pulled the rope with all his might. He didn't know what else he could do but ring the bell.

He had only been a Monk for two years, and had spent all of that time at the Trappist monastery that occupied the top of Barton Hill, overlooking the quaint village of Chumleigh. He never had a reason to visit.

The Order had been there for over a century, but because of some poor investments and dwindling interest, found themselves in irreparable financial trouble, and, despite diversifying into brewing beer, the Monks failed to raise enough money to remain there.

In dire straits, they had agreed to sell the property and the land to a mysterious consortium led by the local MP Tudor Spears. Only a skeleton crew remained to oversee the transition of the grounds, which was due to happen in a few days.

All of that paled into insignificance, and now a solitary question consumed Keating's thoughts. *Was this the end of days?*

His evening had started much like every other. He had been tending to the weeds on the lawn when he first heard echoes of lamentation. The near silence demanded by the order allowed the wailing of the villagers to travel up the hill on the breeze and invade his tranquillity.

Dropping his trowel and compostable bag, Keating looked around for validation of what he was hearing, but he saw only the green lawn and the imposing stonework of the main building itself. He wanted to call out, but knew that regardless of the situation, his actions would be deemed inappropriate at best.

As the sounds of pain grew louder, he rushed back to the small golf cart buggy parked on the gravel driveway nearby and searched under the passenger seat. With a smile, he pulled out a pair of shabby binoculars and praised Father Oliveria for his nerdy pastime of birdwatching.

Keating ran as fast as his robe would allow him along the brow of the hill, alongside the side wall of the monastery, and found a small stone jutting out from the building. Years of built up dirt and grime rubbed against the white of his tunic, but he was finally in position to view the town.

As he scanned the near empty streets, his eyes fell upon the den of iniquity, the pub. A pang of jealousy crashed over him as remembered the nights spent at the Durham student's union, and the activities after, but he regained his resolve and focused on what he could see. His jaw dropped.

It was like Sodom and Gomorrah combined.

Keating threw down the binoculars and ran inside the building, screaming for help. Silence be damned, he thought, before apologising to God. He entered the refectory and ground to a halt. The sight turned his stomach.

He had managed to keep his lunch down, but the stink of defiled flesh made him gag. His hand flew up to his mouth to stifle the noise, but it was too late. The vile creatures who had smote his Brothers noticed his presence.

The desire to flee was overwhelming, and without knowing it, he was out of the building and heading toward the bell tower.

Now inside, and causing an almighty din, his senses returned, and he realised the foolishness of his actions. He released the rope and let the bell ring out a couple more times of its own momentum, and then his fears became reality.

What started off as his sanctuary had become his coffin. Tears formed in the corners of his eyes as a high-pitched creak broke out from the door, which seemed to warp in the limited light.

Through some sort of involuntary reaction, the muscles in his legs tightened, and his skin prickled.

Time appeared to stand still.

It sounded like a whip cracking the floor as the wooden door fissured. Keating didn't wait to see the cracks expanding and the demons that wanted to claim him. He rushed up the wooden staircase that snaked its way up the tower.

As he ran, he resisted the temptation to look back. He didn't have to, as the stench of death was close behind. Closing in. Once at the top, he took a deep breath and glanced down the rickety path that led to hell. It looked like hundreds of those things were scuttling towards him and sounded like more. They were legion.

Keating peered down over the edge at the ground below. He was almost two-hundred feet up. Every second he wasted deciding what to do, those creatures were getting closer. Tears now streamed down his cheeks. He wanted his mum to hold him. To tell him everything was going to be alright.

The incessant sound of death consumed his thoughts. He made the sign of the cross and hauled himself up onto the edge. What he was doing was a mortal sin, but could hell be any worse than what he saw in the refectory?

A smile broke over his face as the smell of freshly cut grass mixed with lavender made its way to him, and he became one with the earth.

CHAPTER 25

"Those poor people," said Russ.

Nita looked at him and sighed. "There's nothing we could have done to help them. There were just too many of those things."

Russ knew she was telling the truth. He also knew that if it wasn't for her, then he would be back there, lying on the street, being eaten by those foul beasts, along with everyone else. Still, it didn't sit right with him. He shouldn't be here, safe and alive. Not at the expense of others who had their whole lives ahead of them. Or at least a few decades anyhow.

"C'mon," said Nita, as she pushed open the heavy door and headed inside Moss Manor. Russ watched her for a moment. He admired how she was remaining so strong despite all this. It was an excellent trait to possess, as long as it was not only on the outside.

He followed her in, glancing at the boarded-up window of the front room as he moved past and into the kitchen. "Cup of tea? Or something stronger?"

"Tea? We can't stay here to drink a cup of tea. We need to get to the quarry and find out if the creatures are coming from there. If they are, then we can…"

"Stop them? What chance have we got? You saw them. How many people like us are now dead? I'm not sure what exactly you want me to do. Look, I'm no spring chicken. I need to rest. My bones ache, my hands are trembling and as for my bladder," said Russ, as he headed to the small toilet at the back of the kitchen.

He returned to find the kettle whistling and Nita pulling two mugs down from a cupboard. He smiled. Perhaps the girl had seen sense. This was beyond them now. Let the police, or better yet, the army, deal with it. Board up the house, relax with a cup of tea and a biscuit. They could even watch Countdown. This was too big for them, and it was time for the young professionals to take over.

Russ sat down at the rounded kitchen table and directed Nita to where the tea, sugar and biscuits were stored. He knew he shouldn't have sugar, not with his diabetes, but extraordinary times and all that. At this stage of his life, what does it matter?

With the freshly brewed liquid steaming out of the hot mugs, Nita sat down and looked at Russ. She lifted the cup in two hands and took a sip. "I've not been entirely honest with you, Russ. I was writing a story about the quarry and how it affected the local community. That much is true. But also, I have a contact in the activist camp and what I really wanted to do was expose the devastating impact on the local wildlife and wider environment."

"So, you understand why we must go to the quarry to see if that is the source of those things? If the quarry somehow caused them to, I don't know."

Russ took a long sip of tea and picked up a biscuit. He placed the snack back down and looked at Nita. "So, you need proof of what these creatures are and where they come from just for a story? You want to risk our lives just so you can see your name in print?

My dear lady, vanity is not a good trait to have, especially not when there are killer monsters out there."

They finished their tea in silence. The only sound being the cracking of a biscuit. *Doc. Pengelly. The officer. Those people at the pub.* The sound of the screaming replayed in Russ's head, and the feeling of helplessness. What would Sofia have told him to do?

He got up from the table and turned on the radio. It was already tuned to Radio Devon.

I've got carpets, beds and furniture,
I've got carpets, beds and furniture,
I've got carpets, beds and furniture,
My name is Mickey Beers

Advert followed advert, until, after nearly switching the blasted contraption off, a local newscast started. More bins knocked over, flooding in Plymouth, drugs in Exeter, and delays reaching some small villages. Nothing about ravenous centipedes in Chumleigh. Perhaps they were trying to avoid a panic. Maybe no one managed to alert the authorities before dying.

"We can't just let this go on, not while we can do something about it,' said Nita, breaking the silence. 'If we do nothing, then more people will die. Even my friend at the camp. Yes, I know it's selfish, and yes, I would get a great story out of this if I survive, but hiding from the world when bad things happen is not the answer. You have to step up, be counted and make a difference. Or at least try."

Russ wondered what this twenty-something knew about stepping up and fighting. He had done his time both on the battlefield and in love, and he was the last one standing. That was not always a blessing, but she was young and will learn that. He doubted she would listen, anyway. Youth was the opportunity to be foolhardy.

He waited before responding, but in those moments, he thought back on what Sofia would say and about how he had acted over the past few years without her, especially since his son's death. It was only a matter of time before the tears started, and if they did, he wasn't sure they would stop. Clenching his jaw, he returned to the radio and turned it off. He remained facing away from Nita. Unable to meet her gaze.

"After my wife's death, the world moved on. Only I didn't want to, but I had my Robert to hold on to. Then he went too, and so I locked myself away, hermetically sealed in my box, and I lived in the past. Sure, people came. Tried to help. But it didn't. I didn't allow it to. So I wallowed in my grief, knowing things had to change but unwilling for them to. And that's how I became who I am now. Sofia would be ashamed at what I've become," said Russ. He turned to face Nita and could see from her eyes that Nita felt genuine sympathy for him. He had lived his life mostly, but wasted the last few years as he waited for death. Now, he had a chance to live again and to help others do it too.

"OK, but you drive," said Russ, and a warmth moved through his body as he saw Nita's face brighten. "First, however, I must pop to the bathroom, and then I have something to show you."

With the last of the whistling noise from the toilet flush, Russ called for Nita to follow him into the garden. They walked towards the large modern shed, where Russ unlocked the padlock and pulled the door open. The light came on automatically and Nita stood there in the doorway, dumbfounded at what was in front of her.

The Land Rover skidded to a stop just short of the quarry entrance, by the side of the makeshift path that led into the woodland and the Extinction Rebellion camp. Russ and Nita each clicked on their Maglite LED torches and moved round to the boot of the vehicle.

"After you," said Russ as he took a step back. He breathed in the fresh country air. It filled his lungs and despite the frigid chill in the air, or perhaps because of it, he felt renewed. He watched by the faint light of the moon as Nita reached into the boot and pulled out a 12-gauge shotgun. Her arms dropped due to the unexpected weight of the contraption, and Russ had to stifle a chuckle. Everyone always picks a weapon too big for them the first time they choose.

"Not only is it heavy, but that one has a bit of a kick. Here, try this," said Russ as he pointed to a Beretta M9. "Or, if you think you are up for it, that," he continued as he signalled toward a Lever Action .223 rifle.

He watched as Nita weighed up her two options and chose the rifle. She loaded up on ammunition, packing spares into her oversized borrowed coat.

"You never really explained why you have all these weapons," said Nita.

"Oh, you know, living out in the country. It's normal," said Russ. He was happy to reveal his familiarity with firearms as he could talk about his time in the military and generally people left it at that, but explaining how he fell in love with Sofia and the complications of her family, not to mention their line of business, was a story he was not willing to tell anyone. It explained the arsenal he had back at his cottage, and he wondered about the questions and the rumours that would circulate once he had passed over to the other side and whoever had the job of clearing his property out found his stash.

The two of them loaded up what they needed.

"What about the rest of this stuff? Do you want to take it?" said Nita.

"Let's leave it here as a backup," said Russ with a smile. "Now, you lead the way as although the light is good here, once we get in them there woods, I'll only have the flashlight and won't be able to see much else. Also, let me know if any of the paths are tricky to walk."

As they set off into the woodlands, Russ noticed that something was off. He knew that his hearing was not fantastic, but the only sound he could pick up was that of their footsteps as they crunched on the dry leaves.

"Stop, you hear that?" said Russ.

"No, what?" Nita froze and tightened her grip on the gun.

"Exactly, where are the sounds of the animals? The insects, owls, anything. Hell, even the activists should be audible from here. It's late, but I can't believe they are all in bed. Get your weapon ready and let's move with caution."

Nita shuffled forward with her rifle raised. Russ was glad at the slower speed the girl was going, but wondered if he should tell her she does not have to swing the gun side to side as she moved. No, let her do it her way, at least while there appeared to be nothing around. But that was the problem. It was eerily quiet, and that was never a good omen.

The smell hit them before they saw the camp. It was Nita who first noticed the strange odour, but it soon pushed past Russ's excessive nose hair, and once he had smelt it, it lingered in his nostrils. He recognised what it meant, but before he could warn Nita, she had rounded the last corner that led to the encampment.

The stench of death was soon mixed with that of vomit as Russ caught up with Nita to find her doubled over and retching until nothing more could come out.

They were too late, but at least their theory was likely to be correct. What little consolation that was.

"We have to check for survivors. Take a moment, breathe, and then we'll go," said Russ. He had seen this type of senseless death before, but someone had to do something and he couldn't do it on his own.

Bloodied bodies laid on mud and leaves. Their clothing was torn and stained. The silence had returned. Russ moved with his trusty 12-gauge ready to secure the perimeter, while Nita pivoted and swung her rifle around like she was in a bad cop show.

Russ wasn't sure which of them heard it first, but the advancing rustling was unmistakable. They fixed their guns on a piece of moving foliage. Their fingers primed on their triggers. Then, movement halfway down the bush. His view wasn't clear, as he couldn't hold the flashlight up alongside the gun, but he didn't need a clear sight with this weapon.

"No," screamed Nita as Russ fired and the shot echoed throughout the night.

The deafening boom was followed by the scream of a man as he flew out from his hiding place. His body hit a tree nearby, and he slumped down. A large hole had punctured his left chest and blood splattered all over the surrounding countryside.

"Fuck," shouted Nita, and she ran towards the dying figure. She cradled him in her arms and screamed something unintelligible at Russ, who remained rooted to the spot. Nita looked down at the man, whose shallow breaths soon stopped. His legs had been torn to shreds, but he must have survived the onslaught somehow.

Why didn't he call out? Jesus, Mary and Joseph, had he killed an innocent man?

Sobbing filled the night for what seemed like an eternity. But when it appeared that grief had swallowed any possibility of the day, another noise sounded out.

CHAPTER 26

The shot rang out against the silence of the night, and Briar froze. He listened. A beat. Then a scream, but not like before. Perhaps his colleagues came through for him.

"Hey you guys, don't shoot, I'm one of you!" said Briar as he moved his way out of the treehouse. He hoped to have been back in the safety of the local pub by now, but his mobile didn't have internet access and the rest of the activists only owned shit that wouldn't help him against those things if they returned. So, he had held his axe close and waited for the cavalry.

He kicked the rope ladder down to the ground and glanced at his saviours. The shadows hid their faces, and when they flashed their lights up in his direction, he had to raise his hands to cover his face from the powerful beams.

"Relax, I'm coming down."

As he began his descent, the euphoria of being saved waned, and logic took control again. *Why hadn't these people identified themselves? There was only a single shot and a scream. What did they shoot?* He pushed the thoughts from his mind. If they were an undercover squad, of course, they wouldn't bloody identify themselves and who cares who they shot. They came here to get him, not those fuckin' soap dodgers he had been living with.

By the time his boots touched solid ground, the two people with torches still had not responded, and he was feeling nervous. He turned to face his saviours but stopped short of facing them as the grisly body of Kit, a teenager who he had shared a joint with just yesterday, laid out on the floor. Bits of his chest splattered on a tree trunk behind.

"What the fuck, he was alright that kid," said Briar. "Still, I know the score, no witnesses. Shall we head to the village?"

"The village isn't safe. What happened here?" It was an unfamiliar voice. It sounded weak. Elderly.

"Wait, who the fuck are you?" said Briar. He continued to move towards the flashlights, the axe still in his hand.

"We're the ones with the guns. Stop there and answer the question?" Continued the man.

"Where's Tobias?" the second one asked. Her voice was a lot younger. Female. Perhaps this wasn't the rescue squad.

"Those things came and killed everyone, or at least I thought they had," said Briar. He glanced back at poor Kit. "So, you aren't the police? Are you going to kill me too?"

"It was an accident!" blurted out the old man. If Briar was to grab a weapon, he would be the easiest of the two. The woman looked small, but she had the energy of youth, and there was no way of knowing how accurate her aim was. Not until it was too late, anyway. Besides, never fuck with an angry bird. He had learned that the hard way. The old guy, though, even if he was good once, his time had passed. Briar turned his body and took a side step toward the geriatric.

"What's your name?" said the girl. Even in the dark, he could see her hands shaking as she held both the gun and the torch cross-armed like they do on TV.

"I'm Jude Briar, a member of the community here. We were just sitting around enjoying the evening when the screaming started and those things ran rampant through the camp. I survived because I was high up and they didn't get to me. I thought I was the only one left." He looked at the poor kid. "I guess I am now."

The geriatric went and sat down on a part of a bench that wasn't covered in blood and rested the shotgun on his lap. The younger one stepped forward towards him.

"I'm Nita. This is Russ. We think the creatures have a nest or whatever in the quarry, and I wanted to ask my friend Tobias if he had seen or heard anything. This, though, answers our question. Now we're going to destroy those fucking creatures."

Briar scoffed. "Are you sure?" He nodded toward Russ, who had his head in his hands and wept. "Let's just head back to civilisation. There's a pub in the village. We can warn people from there."

"We can't. They have ravaged the town. Hopefully, some of them found somewhere safe and called the authorities, but they didn't listen to our cries for help before." said Nita.

"Tell me about it. There's nothing you can do, though, not with him in that state. If the village is done for, we'll just keep going. Plymouth, Exeter, hell let's go to Bristol if you have enough fuel, but it's not safe to wait here."

"Perhaps," said Nita as she made her way toward Russ before sitting down next to him.

Briar watched the unlikely duo hug and considered making a break for their vehicle. He knew how to hot wire a car. That wouldn't be a problem, but what if he gets there and they have no petrol?

It was then as he waited, their blubbering and the annoying mollycoddling, that he noticed the same putrid stench from earlier. He could practically taste the rank odour on his tongue as he spat out what little saliva he had.

"Jude Briar, OK, let's head…"

Briar raised his hand to quiet the girl, and then he moved in a semi-circle, following the slight shift in the rank smell's direction. It was growing in intensity. "Get your guns ready, and let's get the fuck out of here now."

Russ was about to say something, but Briar cut the soppy idiot off. "Stop your boo-hooing. We need to fuckin' leave now!"

Without saying a word, Nita raised her pistol at Briar and fired.

CHAPTER 27

"We can't stop them," said Russ as he sat in his favourite armchair, shivering. A chilly wind whistled through the small gaps at the side of the boards that covered the windows. "I'll have to call someone out in the morning to look at that. If there is anyone left alive to pick up. Maybe I best ring a firm in Plymouth. See if they will travel out for a minor job." Russ sighed.

Nita looked at the broken man. After everything they had been through, it surprised her he had reacted this way. Killing someone would do that, she supposed, but they had come too far, and seen too much death to just give in.

"Here, let me try to get the fire started," said Nita. She had no clue what to do with these old-fashioned fireplaces, having only ever known central heating, but after a few minutes and the coal blackening her hands, she got some heat into the room.

She turned to Russ, whose eyes were barely open. "OK, we don't know much about these things, but we can kill them. We've got the weapons, the location of their lair, and whether or not we like it, we have the responsibility. You aren't to blame for that man's death, but you are now responsible for helping save others. What would your wife and son say?"

Nita braced herself for a verbal onslaught as Russ opened his mouth.

The floorboard in the doorway creaked, and a gruff voice sounded out. "Yeah, you gotta snap out of it, old man." Briar strolled in and placed three cups of tea on the coffee table, taking one for himself.

Russ stared at the stranger, and it was then Nita realised how frail her new friend looked. His skin was paper thin and the areas around his eyes moved from shadow to red at the sides.

The geriatric felt it too and saw the look of pity on Nita's face. He knew they were thinking the same thing. That he should be tucked up in bed, sleeping after a nice cup of cocoa, not being forced into battling a horde of killer centipedes. He also knew what he should be doing. What he *would* be doing if he was younger.

"Tell you what Russ, go get some sleep. Jude and I will take turns watching the house until morning, right?"

Briar spat out his tea and stared at Nita. She saw him rub his nose before he spoke. "Listen, I appreciate you both getting me out of there and stopping that thing before it got me, but I'm not here to babysit you or be a caregiver for him, no offence. If I can use your phone we'll be away from here in no time."

"Aren't you listening? We need to stop them, and the more of us, the better," said Nita.

"Listen, darling. You might have a death wish, but I bloody well don't and I'm certain that grandpa mumbling over there doesn't either. He ain't got long, so why not let him live it?"

Nita felt her blood boil at his cowardice. But was he right? Briar took a slurp of his tea and the sound infuriated Nita. *How could this prick be right?*

"I saw a telephone in the hall," said Briar, and he strolled off before Nita could say anything in return.

Nita turned to Russ and smiled at the old man, who had now fallen asleep in the chair. She walked over to the sofa and pulled the tartan blanket off one of the cushions, but then she heard snippets of the phone call and paused.

"You can't bloody leave me here. I called before. This shit is serious."

"..."

"After everything I've done for you in this job, you're going to hang me out to dry? There's a journalist here, and if you don't extract me immediately, I'll tell her all about Operation Crusty."

"..."

"Fucking cunt. See you in hell."

Nita heard the receiver slam down, and the sharp clang made her gasp. Her eyes darted around and her body stuttered, unsure what the best action would be. She hurried away from the doorway and took hold of the scratchy woollen blanket over Russ. She held it in her hands until Briar returned.

"All OK?" she asked quietly.

"I've been thinking. You saved my life and I owe you, so you get some rest and I'll keep watch."

Nita smiled at the man but wondered what he was up to?

An icy chill ran through Russ's body and he woke in an alerted state. When he realised he was safe at home, his muscles relaxed and he exhaled slowly. He glanced toward the fireplace and half-expected to see Toby curled up and snoring.

"Alright, Gramps. Cuppa?"

Russ turned his head and looked at the strange man from last night. Did he travel back with them? Russ shifted. It was not like him to invite strangers into the house, and now there were two of them.

"Yes, please. I'm sorry, but I forgot your name," said Russ.

"It's Briar. Jude Briar. You take milk? Sugar?"

Russ gave the guest his exact tea order and was happy to not be judged for having three sugars. Diabetes be damned. It also gave him time to think things through. He dreamt of Sofia and she told him to make a difference, and make amends for the death of not only that poor man but the villagers, too. He didn't have long left on this earth, and he would not go out without putting up a fight.

"Thank you," said Russ. He took the mug of almost grey tea. "Where's Nita?"

"Who? Oh the bird, she's still sleeping. I took first watch, but to be honest, it wasn't worth waking her. Now you're up, I'll grab a bit of sleep."

At that moment, a messy-haired Nita entered the room, yawning.

"What time is it?" said Nita.

Russ checked the clock on the mantelpiece. "About six a.m." *No wonder it was still so dark*. "We have a lot to do, so we're going to need a big breakfast. Nita, I'll make yours now, and Jude Briar, is it? Yours will be ready after your nap."

Russ took a final sip of his horrid tea and pulled himself up from his chair. As he straightened up, his back twinged. It was a good thing today was the day, as his joints might not last any longer.

"Does this mean…" said Nita.

Russ smiled and then nodded at her. "Plus, I have a few more surprises in store." He turned to face Briar. "I know you're an environmental activist, but are you familiar with firearms, by any chance?"

The smile he saw on the face of Briar worried Russ, and suggested that this man might not be everything he said he was. Of course, things would go a lot smoother if the man had experience, but there was something off about him.

"Do you not want that bacon? Here, let me help you out," said Russ. He leaned across the table and helped himself to another piece of Nita's full English. The poor girl asked for just a croissant or even toast, but he had refused, saying she would need her strength today, and the only way to ensure that was with a big hearty breakfast.

He was refilling the mugs with tea when, in hushed tones, Nita raised her concerns about the man that was joining them. Russ set down the ceramic teapot in the centre of the table and rubbed the grey stubble on his chin.

"Yes. I have a few doubts myself, but gossip helps no one. Let's focus only on what we know."

"I overheard him on the phone last night, and he knows more than he is letting on. I don't think he's helping us because he has a conscience or wants to save people. There's something else."

"That might well be, but there is never any benefit in worrying about things outside of our control. We simply need to make the best of our situation, and right now we have his help, and we'll need it if we are going to eradicate those beasts. Now, eat up because after this, we have to get to work."

Russ stood up and took his dishes to the sink. "Now, I have some things to prepare before our new guest wakes up."

CHAPTER 28

As the Land Rover pulled up outside the quarry gates, the hard case in the boot crashed into the back of the passenger seat and the thud echoed throughout the inside of the large vehicle.

"It's been too quiet. Think about it. Saturday night and we didn't pass anyone on the way here. There were no lights anywhere. After what you told me, someone would have raised the alarm about what was going on," said Briar.

Russ looked at him but before he could reply saying that there were no other properties on the route, the man asked him what the terrible smell was. "It's the minerals from the quarry. With no one else about, and this breeze, I suppose it's made its way out there."

"It bloody stinks, but at least it ain't those creatures. If the rocks or whatever are giving off that stink, I wonder if someone is working there now?"

"What kind of activist are you? The place has been closed for about a week. The workers all walked out, but I'm not sure why. Officially, it was over pay but with everything that's been going on…," replied Nita. She got out and moved behind the car. She opened the boot and pulled the crate toward her. "You think they knew? This whole time, they've done nothing?"

The two men didn't answer.

"No, probably not, but they might have suspected something was off. It's strange," continued Nita as she unlocked the case and lifted the lid. She glanced back inside the vehicle and noticed that Briar had gone. She looked around the side of the Land Rover and saw him milling by the entrance. "Hey, a little help here," she called in his direction.

"If they aren't working, then why is the gate open?" Briar said.

The three of them pondered on that question, and Russ couldn't offer a single reason why it would be open if there wasn't anyone there. He stepped down from the driver's side and joined Nita behind the car. Briar followed soon after.

The sun had long since set, yet a strange, dark red hue lingered on the horizon. Russ zipped up his fleece jacket and thought if they were looking at it out over the water instead of this man-made destruction of nature, it would have been beautiful.

"OK, I doubt there is anyone working, but let's play it safe and stick close to one another. Keep your eyes peeled and if there is any danger, we'll spot it first. Let's adapt to whatever we find," said Russ. He could sense that the tension was building.

"You've got me out here, risking my skin. Don't you reckon we should have a better plan than see what happens?" said Briar as he rubbed his hands together and stepped from his left to his right foot and back again.

Russ nodded but considered the man's response and tone. He was certain that they were being joined by a guy who lacked the patience to appreciate nature, to accept the natural order of things and the lack of control that comes with it. A man who needed tasks set out for him, and for action or perhaps even some sort of gratification, to be around every corner. His whole demeanour seemed at odds with someone who was an environmentalist. "You're right, but we are going into the unknown and we need to be prepared for anything. Besides, I've never been into this place before, and I doubt you two know the layout either. Although, as a member of that group, you might have scoped it out. What were you protesting again?"

The man looked to the side briefly before returning to meet Russ's gaze. The generic reply he offered was exactly as Russ expected. It was one that would have appeased most people with a passing interest or knowledge, but Russ wasn't like everyone else. In his past, he had dealt with a lot of different individuals and knew when someone had a secret or two. Although it was not clear what part of his life he was not divulging. That was also something Russ was all too familiar with.

"Let's just focus on the here and now. Right, are you guys ready? Choose your weapons," said Nita, with an enormous smile on her face.

Russ and Briar, standing to either side of her, looked down at the array of firearms which Nita had laid out in the car's boot. Briar wolf whistled, and Russ snuck a sideways look and noted how the man wasn't phased by the killing machines in front of him.

"Jude, you said you know how to use a gun, didn't you?" said Russ.

"Of course. I mean, yeah, I'm familiar. I used to own a BB pistol when I was younger."

"Well, these are a little more powerful, but something tells me you'll get the hang of them pretty quickly. Pick whatever you two need, but leave the 12 gauge for me. That's this one, in case you were wondering," said Russ, looking at Briar.

In silence, they all checked their guns and packed additional ammunition wherever they could fit it.

"One more thing, Nita, would you mind going to the glove box and taking out the torches that are in there, and there is something else I think which might come in handy."

The two men headed to the entrance as Russ told Briar about the history of the local topography.

Nita pulled out the flashlights, and the small, wrapped bundle beside them. She unwrapped the cloth, exposing the contents. "What the fuck?"

CHAPTER 29

A thin fog quickly rolled in over the hills and cloaked the quarry in a blanket of gloom. The powerful Maglite torches of the group barely penetrated through the shifting grey matter as they made their way toward the open pit that dominated the area.

Russ felt the stone shuffle underneath his feet as the light droplets of rain patted his jacket. The weather was going to play a part in how things panned out. He just didn't know how. Thunder roared in the distance.

He looked at his colleagues in this endeavour. Briar wore an indeterminable expression, but Nita, her face illuminated in the blue light of a mobile phone, was putting her emotions out there for all to see.

"There won't be any signal out here, Nita," said Russ.

"There's no bloody signal in this whole godforsaken area. The sooner they roll out nationwide 5G, the better. Anyway, it's not the phone I'm using, but the camera. It has a night mode, but it's pretty bloody useless if you actually want to use it at night. Can anyone make anything out down there?" said Nita as she angled her mobile over the abyss.

"The only way we will know what's down there is to see for ourselves. Come on," replied Russ. The thunder sounded closer and with it, the rain grew in strength.

"We best be quick. We don't want to be stuck down there if this weather keeps up." Russ shouted, worried that the pummelling rain would drown him out. He started down the winding track without waiting for a reply.

"What do you mean? If it's dangerous, we gotta turn back and head to a city for help," said Briar. He turned to Nita. "You're a journalist. I'm sure you could kick up a stink about all this."

"Even journalists need evidence. If I can't prove what is going on, the government and big business will just cover all this up. C'mon."

"Fine. As soon as we get some evidence, though, we're gone. I ain't drowning down in this godforsaken hole!"

After walking downhill for forty minutes, Russ's hamstrings ached more than he ever thought possible, but he had made it to the bottom without falling and he was glad for that. The rain had also stopped, leaving a low pool of standing water on the floor of the pit.

"Now what?" said Briar.

With sagged shoulders, Russ looked around the dull, grey landscape. Silhouettes of large rectangular objects obscured the distance, while the dirty yellow of a crane cab made itself visible through the gloom.

No one said anything, but in the silence Russ sensed something. How he heard it he couldn't be sure, but the gentle sound worked its way into his brain. Then he realised what he was hearing. The water was flowing. He walked forward, following the light flow, before stopping a short distance ahead of the others.

Briar and Nita followed him and the three of them, now standing side-by-side, stared down as the water continued to work its way around their boots and down to a central point. The reason opened up in front of them.

"You think that's it?" said Nita. She moved closer to the edge. "You guys hear that? It's a hissing sound."

The water cascaded down a sharp drop, taking dirt and mud with it. The insidious noise from beneath grew in intensity and Russ realised what they were hearing. He took a step back and readied his shotgun.

"Fall back," he murmured.

The others didn't move.

"Fall back," said Russ again. This time louder. His throat was raw with the exertion. All the while, the hissing grew intenser and more sustained.

"What are you talking about?" said Briar. His eyes widened as long stalk-like objects protruded out of the hole in the ground. "Fuck!"

"To the nearest cabin," said Russ. His voice cracked as he gave the order and ran as fast as he could. The mud was slippery, and he struggled to keep his balance. He knew if those things came for him, he would have no chance. His lungs narrowed and a burning sensation overtook his chest. Within fifty yards, he doubled over. He wheezed and tried to suck in any air he could.

Was this it? Russ wanted to laugh at his foolish dreams of going out with a bang. He closed his eyes and cleared his mind of all but one thing.

Gunfire echoed around the stone amphitheatre and snapped Russ out of his reverie. He steeled himself, took a series of deep breaths, and faced the tide. Nita and Briar now stood on either side of him. The muzzle flash of their weapons momentarily blinded Russ but he realised that the strange activist was more than competent with a weapon. Russ glanced to his right and spotted a group of large centipedes advancing on Nita's flank. He hoisted up the 12 gauge and let fire, killing two and scattering the rest. Nita looked at him and gave a thankful smile.

"We'll never make it," said Briar. "There's too many of them. We still have enough bullets for ourselves, though."

"Don't you talk like that, soldier,'" said Russ. "Nita, pass me that something extra from the glove box."

Nita handed over the item. "Is this safe?"

Russ smiled. "Just get ready."

He unwrapped the cloth, taking out one red stick, and then withdrew a Zippo lighter from his top. His thumb flicked the wheel. The flame met the fuse of the stick and sizzled.

"Move," said Russ as he lobbed the dynamite toward the conveyor belt of centipedes that spewed out from the ground.

Nita and Briar fired off a final round before they all ran. The boom of the explosion filled the night, and the impact caused the earth to tremble. Nita looked back and watched as, in their confusion, the routed creatures crashed into each other before retreating to their foul subterranean lair.

CHAPTER 30

The door of the cabin was already open when they reached it, and seemed safe enough, but Nita and Briar still searched the room as Russ kept watch. Once they felt secure and the immediate threat had reduced, that was when the mistakes would creep in, thought Russ. He had seen it all before.

"Grab that desk and slide it behind the door," said Briar as he and Nita continued to search for weak spots.

"We have to go on the offensive. They are all together at the moment. Scared. We will not get another chance like this," said Russ.

"Another chance? I hate to break it to you, pops, but we just had it. It's over. Did you see how many of those fucking things there are? Too bloody many. If we don't hunker down here, we'll never get another chance to have a pint or a fuck," said Briar. He moved over to a large filing cabinet and dragged it toward the entrance. "If I'm moving this. At least make yourself useful and find a fuckin' phone."

"No, Russ is right. This is all pointless. Even if there is a working phone in here, if they attack again, then it'll be too late by the time help arrives. If we barricade the door, they'll smash through the windows. If we somehow block them too, then they will just find another way. Back in the pub, they seemed to come from everywhere," said Nita.

"Shut up and follow orders. Old man, don't make me ask again. Look for the fucking phone."

Russ moved through the Tardis-like cabin and his eyes swept the three desks arranged nearer the back. Photographs of families, stacks of paper with order quantities and safety reports, but no telephones. Not even a walkie talkie or a CB radio. He looked at Briar and shook his head. The man's reaction told him everything he needed to know about who Jude Briar was, underneath his hippy facade.

Russ wasn't sure if it was the swearing or the noise of the filing cabinet receiving a kicking that startled him the most, but he was certain more now than ever that just doing nothing was a death sentence. He had been lucky to survive so far, but for what?

It was as if Nita had read his mind when she asked him how much dynamite he had left over. Three more sticks. That question was understandable, but the next, which he would find out was integral to her plan, confused him.

"You are fucking mad. We don't have enough ammunition to get rid of those things. We've tried. If you don't want to stay here, then let's make a run for it and leave it to be someone else's problem," said Briar, interrupting the conversation.

"Look, we know we can't stay here, but running is not an option. You've seen how fast they can move, we wouldn't all make it to the top without being swarmed," said Nita in a low tone as she glanced across the cabin toward Russ who was sitting in an office chair on the other side of the room and rubbing his feet.

"Not all of us, no," said Briar, following her gaze. "But you and me can, and I'm sure at his age he won't mind sacrificing his last few weeks or months, if it means we live. If you ask him, I think he'll agree. He seems sweet on you, and I see why."

"What did you say? It sounded like you said to use Russ as bait so we can live our happy lives together in bed. I would rather take my chance out there with those creatures than go on a date with a creep like you." Nita turned and called over to Russ, asking him to get ready and join them. Out of the corner of her eye, she saw the smirk on Briar's face and her stomach turned.

The two men stood there looking at Nita, and despite everything, she was empowered. Although perhaps now was not the time to be feeling good about herself. A few days ago she was just Nita, the junior reporter who made the tea, reported on bins falling over in storms and was seen as different from the rest of the office. But now she was the only one with a plan and about to make a real difference. A life or death decision that affected them all. She noticed her left leg was trembling, and she hoped the others didn't notice. She cleared her throat.

"Right, it's likely we aren't making it out of here alive. There *is* only one way, and that is what we spoke about earlier. To fight. None of us can work a crane, but it can't be too difficult to get it to do what we want. I need someone to lift me over the centre of that crack in the earth. Then I'll throw the sticks of dynamite down. As soon as I let go of the last stick, you swing me back to solid ground and we all run like hell. It's not those things that will be dangerous to us, but the risk of a sinkhole. So, which one of you wants to take the crane and who wants to provide cover?"

Russ and Briar remained staring at her, only now ashen faced. When she had asked them earlier about whether they had ever used a crane, she noticed the confusion on their faces, but it was now the only way.

Sure, they could get to the edge of the hole and throw the dynamite down, but there was no guarantee those creatures wouldn't burst forth and devour them before they got away. Or even that the dynamite would go deep enough to destroy them. This is their only chance and they need to take it.

"No, no, my dear, that is too dangerous. I might not have a firm grip nowadays, but send me over that Hellmouth. I know how to use the dynamite. You may throw it too soon or worse yet, too late. Besides, if anything should go wrong, it is better for it to go awry with me than you," said Russ.

"Yeah, what he said," said Briar.

Nita thought she could smell the stench of perspiration on the paper activist, but perhaps it was cowardice. It surprised her when Russ spoke, appraising the man's natural sharpshooting skills and suggesting he take point, leaving Nita to work out the crane. She had won several prizes on the claw machines at funfairs and arcades, including a Gameboy at some arcade in Dawlish Warren.

She could handle this. Couldn't she?

CHAPTER 31

It had only taken a couple of moments to reach the crane, but what appeared to be a minor exertion for the others was a herculean effort for Russ, who could feel his heart pounding, his muscles aching and a damp sweat under his warm clothing. Was it simply the physical movement causing it, or something else? When was his last meal? As the group stopped beside the enormous machine, Russ reached into his jacket pocket and pulled out his emergency mints. The sugary effect wouldn't last long, but hopefully long enough.

There was an incoherent mumbling echoing in the background, and Russ found the other two looking at him. His head was pounding, as if someone was playing the drums inside his cranium, and he struggled to concentrate on the noise coming out of Nita's mouth. When she paused, Russ nodded. Now was not the time to let the group down.

He felt Briar's hands drag him toward the crane's hook, which had already been lowered to the floor, and attach a cord around his waist.

"It's the best I could find. If it starts to dig into you, then wiggle it a little but keep it firmly attached. The discomfort is a lot better than the alternative," said Briar, as he secured each of Russ's ankles to the attached hook. "You'll need your hands free, but I'd still advise you to keep hold with all your strength for as long as possible. Tell you what though, you got some balls, old man."

The two men shared only a solemn nod. It was then, as Briar retreated to the cab, that the hydrogen sulphide fumes seemed to get stronger and Russ's head went light. What had he agreed to?

"You worked out what you're doing, little lady?" hollered Briar as the crane's engine spluttered into life, filling the almost cavernous space with a dull, rhythmic pulse.

Nita looked down at the man shouting at her, back at the control panels, her brow furrowed. After a moment, she replied she was ready.

Briar pulled up his jacket collar and turned to watch the trembling old man attached to the crane hook. "He's gonna bruise like a peach," he mumbled.

The wind whistled between Russ's ear hair as he clung onto the metallic cord and swung side-to-side over the gaping crack. He glanced down into the swirling abyss and swallowed the rising lump in his throat. After sucking in a deep breath, he closed his eyes and waited for the nausea to pass.

"Now, throw it now!"

The scream broke through the clanking of the crane, the hum of the wind, and the incessant hissing. Russ opened his eyes and watched as the darkness appeared to shift within itself. He focused on the writhing sheets of black and then realised what he was looking at.

His palm was sweaty and his grip loosened, yet somehow his fingers remained stiff and refused to bend back around the metal he was gripping for dear life. He steeled himself, leaned down into the middle of the pit of giant centipedes, which were crawling on top of each other in order to breach the surface, with those highest up scaling the vertical rock face and pouring out of the hole. Russ freed a hand, thankful not to hear the certain cracking of his bones, and hooked the cable in the crook of his elbow. He puffed out frigid air and prayed for his success.

Briar fired off three shots, sending the first few of the foul creatures back into the darkness, but there were too many pouring forth out of the cold, wet ground. He took a step and fired another shot. Then he repeated the entire process, giving himself a moment to steal a look across at the crane.

Russ made eye contact with the strange activist, but his attention shifted as a shrill scream cut through the air. *Nita.* The crane jerked forward and Russ jolted as it yanked him upwards. He regained some purchase on the wire and realised the centipedes were flinging themselves at the hook, swinging just beneath his feet.

He glanced around his surroundings. Hundreds and hundreds of the things now filled the walls. The near deafening roar of gunfire echoed throughout the quarry and Russ returned to reality and the task at hand.

A hail of bullets erupted from Briar's semi-automatic rifle, sending a wave of centipedes back down into the pit from which they came. Some squealed in pain, but most hurtled into nothingness with their cries lost in oblivion.

Russ ground his teeth and released his grip. He swung out like a pirate swinging off a mast and reached an arm inside his coat. Holding the stick of dynamite in one hand, he fished out the lighter with the other, while staying upright, and lit the fuse.

Three... two... one.

He let go of the fizzing stick and watched it fall into the mass of arthropods. The darkness consumed the sharp flame.

"Pull me out, Nita," yelled Russ. "Pull me out now!"

Nita pointed the pistol out of the small side window and fired off pot shots at the advancing creatures. Her first two missed their mark, but the third slug split the orange shell that covered one of the leg segments. But the creature kept moving. Its soft flesh exposed and leaking a disgusting fluid.

"Now!" screamed Russ. He braced himself to take the impact and for the explosion to consume his body.

Briar looked at the crane to see what was causing the delay. His eyes bulged as he saw the bottom of the cab crawling with the creatures. He turned back towards Russ, who by now was swinging over the gap, which continued to vomit forth the hideous monsters.

He raised his gun.

CHAPTER 32

Mud splashed under Briar's heavy boots as he moved forward. Step-by-step he was getting closer to the inundated cab. His shoulder burned as he controlled the recoil from the semi-automatic rifle as he fired shot after shot.

By the time he had taken out five or six of the creatures, he stopped counting and entered a flow state where the wind, cold and shouting of his colleagues all drifted into the background.

The sludge under his feet soon gave way to the crunch and squelch of centipede bodies as he continued to decimate the never ending horde.

Click. Click. Click.

As if sensing the danger, the fresh wave of centipedes made for the alpha, while the survivors stopped their siege of Nita in the crane cab and turned their attention to their new foe who had now knelt down to reload his weapon.

Nita swung open the door and screamed at Russ. "I can't move it. The crane's not working."

The gigantic creatures sensed the vulnerability, and swarmed en masse, back toward the crane and the exposed warm bodies. Nita screamed and retreated into the cab just before the first pair of legs reached it.

Briar stared at the winding path that led away from the quarry, but his eyes were drawn back to the crane. A roar erupted from his throat and he made his way toward his new friends.

He swung a boot and connected with the mid-section of the first centipede he came upon, sending it flying into the night and crashing into another of its foul horde. As he reached the cab, he thrust the butt of the rifle into the chitinous shield of a creature and shattered its body.

"Get the job done," screamed Briar.

Nita nodded and shoved the crane claw lever in all directions, and as the machine whirled into action, Russ swung around once again.

Briar turned to provide cover fire but was too late as a giant, white centipede scuttled up his leg. He swung his weapon down, but the creature curled around his thigh and avoided the blow. A burning sensation spread out from his leg.

He fell back into the side of the cab and lost his grip on the rifle. The pain seared its way through his body, and he gritted his teeth. His cheek pressed up against the cold metal, and he lifted his eyes up to glimpse Nita. He didn't know why, but he wanted to make sure she was safe. Then he registered her screams. A centipede had squirmed a quarter of its body through a slight gap between the window frame and the window. Ignoring the pain, Briar reached out a hand and grabbed the bottom legs of the creature. His fingers only covered part of the creature's girth and it wriggled free of his grasp.

Briar swung a shoulder and used the momentum to grab the centipede with both hands. He yanked as hard as he could. His head was light and his balance gone. The world became a blurred patchwork of colours and he crashed down into the mud. His arms splayed out, releasing his prey. A sickening crack sounded out as the spine of the foul monster still wrapped around his leg shattered into pieces.

The released centipede flew up into the air and gravity brought it back down directly onto Briar's face. Dirt and secreted juice slid onto his tongue. The creature wriggled itself into an upright position and encircled Briar's neck. It squeezed as tight as an anaconda.

He puffed his cheeks out and then grimaced. Clarity returned, if only for a second, as the upper portion of the centipede in his hands flopped down through the air, as if in slow motion.

Briar opened his mouth wide to scream. His brain, or what was left functioning of it anyway, begged him not to, but it was too late. The cavity was filled with the mandibles of the horrible thing that forced itself further inside. It first stretched the flesh at the side of Briar's mouth, dislodging teeth as it moved, and then wriggled its way down through the upper throat until becoming stuck in the bloated human canal.

Nita watched in horror as the stench of death creeped into the cab and overpowered her senses. She trembled as she watched the grotesque animal defile Briar's body and was thankful when the sight became hidden under a sea of wriggling creatures. A sea whose levels continued to rise until the cab itself was under threat of being submerged.

Russ withdrew the last stick of dynamite with one hand and held on to the swinging wire for dear life with the other. His vision was blurred, but as he swung around in a three-hundred-and-sixty degree arc, he recognised the scurrying forms coming towards him over the beam that connected the crane cab to the hoist. Fortune favoured the brave, he told himself, and he let go of the cable and fumbled in his pocket for the lighter.

He flicked open the lid and spun the flint wheel. Only a flicker of light. He glanced at the line of ever closer creatures and tried again. A spark erupted, only to be distinguished by the breeze caused by his swirling movement.

Two centipedes had positioned themselves directly above him, their antennae swinging wildly. Russ looked up as he turned the wheel one last time. He saw only the firm, off-yellow underside momentarily before it pushed his nose to the side. Blood gushed out through his nostrils. While the creature continued its descent down into the pit.

The second centipede lowered itself down and Russ felt its rough feet as they tentatively explored and then gained purchase on the back of his neck. He stiffened at the touch, but the lighter remained lit.

"Our Father, who art in heaven…" muttered Russ, as he wriggled his legs, and tried to kick with all his might. With the movement, his right foot came loose from its bonds.

Then the earth shook.

CHAPTER 33

Chunks of flesh, matter and gore erupted upward in a plume of viscera before the inevitable gravitational pull caused it to rain down like a bombing raid.

Nita watched as the mosaic of centipedes that covered the cab windows collapsed into a bloody pile. Some creatures had their grip broken by the falling pieces of their comrades. The separated limbs and lumps of their elderly nemesis pummelled others. Meanwhile, any survivors scuttled away in fear as the ground shook ever more violently and grumbled like an old man sending soup back at a deli.

The groaning of metal being bent past its point of endurance invaded the cab, and Nita felt a slight shift in her balance. Through the gaps made by the fleeing centipedes, she just made out the mouth of the initial crack, becoming ever wider. The now yawning chasm was waking up and looking to devour everything in its path. And that meant her.

She checked her pistol, although she had to admit she didn't know what she was checking for, and kicked the cab door open, surprising two baby centipedes, and they flung out into the cold air before crashing to the muddy ground with a plop.

Nita moved forward with purpose but paused as the door swung back with violent force and nearly smacked her in the face. She jumped at the near-miss and a yelp made its way from her throat. After taking a breath, she pushed the door open and raised the pistol.

Her eyes darted around the immediate area, scanning for threats, but they had not yet adjusted for the darkness and so they missed the closeness of the void. It was only when she went to step down from the crane cab steps, and she fell face first into the dirt, that her proximity to sudden death hit her. In a single beat it dragged the whole crane behind her down into oblivion.

An involuntary release of urine warmed her jeans but also snapped her out of the shock of the impact. With an almost animal instinct she flung her arms forwards and kicked her legs, scrambling with all her might away from the encroaching death.

Survival took over her thoughts and her body shut down anything that could not help it achieve that goal. The horrors of the hellish creatures and what they had done would be dealt with later, but first she had to make sure there was a later. And to do that, she had to move. Fast. It was the only way.

She pushed her palms into the sloppy ground and raised her feet so only her toes connected with the ground. As she prepared to push forward, she noticed a movement in the corner of her eye. She tensed her leg muscles as something approached.

Nita wasn't sure if she had screamed out loud or only in her mind, but the feeling drowned out the rest of her thoughts as she pushed onwards. Explosive power burst out from her muscles and she propelled herself forward. She did not dare stop or look around; instead her eyes focused on a fixed point in the distance and nothing could break her determination. Behind her, the ground gave way and the lower segments of the baby centipedes, out for vengeance, dipped and then swung down, pulling the front segments with them and hurtling the animals into the darkness.

She sprinted up the winding path and continued even as her lungs burned and everything became fuzzy. As if she was living in an impressionist painting. Her legs refused to stop until she reached the safety of the Land Rover, where she launched herself into the driver's side, turned the keys that were left in the ignition, and stared at the illuminated ground ahead of her.

Then she burst into tears.

CHAPTER 34

"How much are you offering?" said Nita. This was the seventh phone call she had received that morning, requesting an exclusive interview and the opportunity to tell her side of the story. As if there was another side.

She glanced out of the front bay room window and contemplated if any of the offers were sincere. Most simply wanted her to add the freak part to their show. Good for ratings, no doubt.

After a few days of sobbing, sleeping and, if she's honest, over drinking, Nita got things straight in her mind. Selling her story was the only thing that would help her. She felt bad about it, profiting off the death of those people, especially Russ, but she needed money and without explaining to her work why she had gone silent for half of the week, she also required a new job. After being laughed at by the first couple of mainstream channels, she gave up hope and posted the evidence online.

It took less than two hours before the British government became aware of this viral sensation and refuted the claims. They arranged for an "expert" to contact the digital publications and denounce the photographs as obvious fakes.

Word spread throughout the industry and the social media channels of this weird attention seeking girl, so recently sacked from her job as a fledgling reporter, and Nita was certain her hopes of a career were gone.

It was then the telephone calls started. They came from conspiracy sites, oddball YouTube presenters, and the Channel Five TV station. She took the latter. It was a lunchtime segment on some talk show or other. The money wasn't great, but it would at least cover the rent that month. Especially now because she couldn't return to her parents' home. They still hadn't forgiven her decision to study journalism instead of pharmacy, so they certainly would not accept this latest *shame* in a hurry.

"Welcome, Nita, it's fantastic to have you on the show today," said Richard Partridge, the show's presenter.

Nita looked around the sparse audience and the makeshift set and doubted she had made the right decision. It had taken almost four hours by train to get to London, of which she had to stand for three. Then there was another crowded journey on the underground. All the time, a voice in the back of her head told her this was a mistake. She didn't listen, but she did chew her fingernails the entire way.

Now sat in the studio, she moved her hands under her thighs, glanced at Richard, and said hello.

"The footage you took is fascinating, but what do you say to those who have said that it looks more like a cheap horror film than a real-life situation? Is this a War of the Worlds style hoax?"

"I don't know what that is, but this isn't a joke. It happened. What do you all think happened to that village? Where is everyone?"

"It's OK," said Richard, with his hands up. He glanced off screen and asked if someone could get the woman a glass of water. "Now, you have been through a terrible ordeal, and we have a surprise in store for you! Meet Dr Greg Palmer, a specialist in PTSD."

The small middle-aged crowd clapped their appreciation as a man in an ill-fitting brown suit strode out and sat down next to her. He waffled on about shock and how, in this case, a fantastical story had been created in order to deal with a very real trauma.

"Of course it's real. I'm not making it up!"

"No, no, I didn't mean to imply you were lying. Only that we, as humans, have divergent interpretations. The way in which we process difficult situations is not uniform. What we do know, however, was that there was a major gas leak in the village, and the subsequent explosion caused the tragedy which wiped out the inhabitants. Or so we thought until you came forward. That is a fact."

"You have no memory of this horrible incident, and that's normal. So, in these circumstances, your brain needs to account for the lost time and…"

Nita had heard enough. She tore off her lapel microphone and stormed off.

Sitting in Paddington Station, Nita flicked listlessly through the Metro newspaper as she waited for her train to come in. The headlines were a blur of ink and shapes. Until one caught her attention.

"Quarry in devastated Devon village due to reopen under new management, thanks to emergency worker visas sponsored by local MP."

CHAPTER 35

The ancient rock groaned as it shifted. The friction of the movement produced long fissures that cracked and opened up. Stone cascaded down into the British channel, and with it, an abandoned cavern developed a fresh opening.

Sensing a meal, a seagull swooped down and glided into the blackness of the new cave. Its wings brushed against flimsy stalactites that swayed with its impact. The gull let out a harrowing squawk as one of the hanging obstacles used its momentum to release from the ceiling and land on the lower half of the large bird.

In the darkness, the strange subterranean monster wrapped its legs around the gull and dug its maxillipeds into the winged creature, causing it to crash into the ground. Tens of centipedes swarmed the body and stripped it of its flesh.

Those which were pushed aside or could not reach the comatose bird turned toward the breeze. They scuttled out into the early morning sun, down the jagged rock face and into the Plymouth sound where the gentle wake of a paddle boarder who was out too far caught their attention.

The End

Check out other great

Cryptid Novels!

P.K. Hawkins

THE CRYPTID FILES

Fresh out of the academy with top marks, Agent Bradley Tennyson is expecting to have the pick of cases and investigations throughout the country. So he's shocked when instead he is assigned as the new partner to "The Crag," an agent well past his prime. He thinks the assignment is a punishment. It's anything but.Agent George Crag has been doing this job for far longer than most, and he knows what skeletons his bosses have in the closet and where the bodies are buried. He has pretty much free reign to pick his cases, and he knows exactly which one he wants to use to break in his new young partner: the disappearance and murder of a couple of college kids in a remote mountain town.Tennyson doesn't realize it, but Crag is about to introduce him to a world he never believed existed: The Cryptid Files, a world of strange monsters roaming in the night. Because these murders have been going on for a long time, and evidence is mounting that the murderer may just in fact be the legendary Bigfoot.

Gerry Griffiths

DOWN FROM BEAST MOUNTAIN

A beast with a grudge has come down from the mountain to terrorize the townsfolk of Porterville. The once sleepy town is suddenly wide awake. Sheriff Abel McGuire and game warden Grant Tanner frantically investigate one brutal slaying after another as they follow the blood trail they hope will eventually lead to the monstrous killer. But they better hurry and stop the carnage before the census taker has to come out and change the population sign on the edge of town to ZERO.

🐦 @severedpress
f /severedpress

Check out other great

Cryptid Novels!

J.H. Moncrieff

RETURN TO DYATLOV PASS

In 1959, nine Russian students set off on a skiing expedition in the Ural Mountains. Their mutilated bodies were discovered weeks later. Their bizarre and unexplained deaths are one of the most enduring true mysteries of our time. Nearly sixty years later, podcast host Nat McPherson ventures into the same mountains with her team, determined to finally solve the mystery of the Dyatlov Pass incident. Her plans are thwarted on the first night, when two trackers from her group are brutally slaughtered. The team's guide, a superstitious man from a neighboring village, blames the killings on yetis, but no one believes him. As members of Nat's team die one by one, she must figure out if there's a murderer in their midst—or something even worse—before history repeats itself and her group becomes another casualty of the infamous Dead Mountain.

Gerry Griffiths

CRYPTID ZOO

As a child, rare and unusual animals, especially cryptid creatures, always fascinated Carter Wilde. Now that he's an eccentric billionaire and runs the largest conglomerate of high-tech companies all over the world, he can finally achieve his wildest dream of building the most incredible theme park ever conceived on the planet... CRYPTID ZOO. Even though there have been apparent problems with the project, Wilde still decides to send some of his marketing employees and their families on a forced vacation to assess the theme park in preparation for Opening Day. Nick Wells and his family are some of those chosen and are about to embark on what will become the most terror-filled weekend of their lives—praying they survive. STEP RIGHT UP AND GET YOUR FREE PASS... TO CRYPTID ZOO

 SEVEREDPRESS

 @severedpress
/severedpress

Check out other great

Cryptid Novels!

Hunter Shea

LOCH NESS REVENGE

Deep in the murky waters of Loch Ness, the creature known as Nessie has returned. Twins Natalie and Austin McQueen watched in horror as their parents were devoured by the world's most infamous lake monster. Two decades later, it's their turn to hunt the legend. But what lurks in the Loch is not what they expected. Nessie is devouring everything in and around the Loch, and it's not alone. Hell has come to the Scottish Highlands. In a fierce battle between man and monster, the world may never be the same. Praise for THEY RISE : "Outrageous, balls to the wall...made me yearn for 3D glasses and a tub of popcorn, extra butter!" – The Eyes of Madness "A fast-paced, gore-heavy splatter fest of sharksploitation." The Werd "A rocket paced horror story. I enjoyed the hell out of this book." Shotgun Logic Reviews

BAKER COUNTY
BIGFOOT
CHRONICLE

C.G. Mosley

BAKER COUNTY BIGFOOT CHRONICLE

Marie Bledsoe only wants her missing brother Kurt back. She'll stop at nothing to make it happen and, with the help of Kurt's friend Tony, along with Sheriff Ray Cochran, Marie embarks on a terrifying journey deep into the belly of the mysterious Walker Laboratory to find him. However, what she and her companions find lurking in the laboratory basement is beyond comprehension. There are cryptids from the forest being held captive there and something...else. Enjoy this suspenseful tale from the mind of C.G. Mosley, author of Wood Ape. Welcome back to Baker County, a place where monsters do lurk in the night!

Printed in Great Britain
by Amazon

83047363R00081